FINDING DANI

ONCE A MARINE, ALWAYS A MARINE - BOOK 3

KORI DAVID

COKEA, LLC

Finding Dani
By: Kori David

This is an original publication of CoKeA, LLC.

Copyright © 2019 by Kori David
ISBN 978-0-9960623-6-7

Printed in the United States of America.

www.KoriDavid.com

❀ Created with Vellum

For my daughter, Jamie, who is a crusader herself and wants to help solve crime by becoming a Forensic Pathologist. Reach for the stars, my love. You can and will be whatever you decide to be. And for my son, Cole, who has no idea what he wants to be when he decides to grow up. I am so proud of my little boy who is learning so many lessons to become a good, strong, man.
I love you both to the moon and back.

CHAPTER 1

"*I*t's a good thing I don't own a gun," Dr. Danielle Bordeaux said, as she batted at the Satan-spawned horsefly busily driving her insane.

"I think a flyswatter would do the trick," said Claire Belgarde, the woman sharing Dani's 'office.' "A really big one."

Dani stopped writing again and glared at the insect. "I'm not sure an Uzi would do the trick on this thing." She'd been all over the world, but there was something about Africa that seemed to make the flies bigger and more aggressive.

"I thought you were a pacifist?"

Turning back to her writing, Dani decided to ignore that as well as the snicker that came with it. In general, she was, but she harbored a deep hatred of bugs, no matter how many legs or wings they had. Even butterflies weren't above suspicion.

"Tell me what you miss the most today," Claire asked.

"Air conditioning," Dani said with a small smile, knowing she was being distracted. How Claire managed to stay cheerful in the worst circumstances amazed her. She was obnoxiously upbeat.

"Yesterday you missed chocolate the most."

"What was the day before?"

She didn't hesitate. "Flushing toilets."

Dani shook her head. Claire had one of those memories—the kind that came in handy most of the time, but could be a destructive weapon when she was pissed.

"What's the name of this village again?"

Claire stood at the back of the tent, cataloguing slides and samples. She paused and then spelled it out. "I can never pronounce it correctly."

This time the CDC had sent them to a village in south Guinea, Africa, to investigate and eradicate a strand of the Ebola virus that had ravaged the inhabitants of the area. It was day twenty-eight of a thirty day stint; the Ebola was gone, and Dani and her team were ready to go home for some rest. Although the infected had been symptom-free for two weeks, they had lost nearly half the village.

Something Dani couldn't get past. She was a doctor, damn it. And, ridiculous as it was, and unrealistic, she took each death personally.

"I want a real bath. Not a bucket shower, but hot water in an actual tub with bubbles and some chilled white wine. And maybe a hot guy who desperately wants to shave my legs for me," Claire said.

"That sounds like heaven."

Dani stood to stretch some of the kinks out of her lower back when they heard the yelling. Raw and intense.

Terrified.

All the hair stood up on her arms and her heart rate sped up at the screaming. *What the hell?* She shot a look at her friend and stepped outside.

The sun was starting its descent, but the light outside

was still good. A small breeze kicked up dust and blew the smell of cooking meat toward her. She hoped to God that it wasn't more fruit bats. That plague was helping spread Ebola from village to village. Tests had proven that bats from this area tested positive for the virus.

"Dani, we have to go," Travis Millet panted as he skidded to a stop next to her. He was out of breath from running and sweat dripped from under his bush hat down the sides of his tanned face.

Travis was one of the best contact tracers the CDC employed and had been with Dani and Claire for several deployments now. He had the uncanny ability to find all friends and relatives that may have come into contact with infected patients. Usually within twenty-four hours, which was vital for containment.

"Deep breaths," she said.

Reaching out, she touched his shoulder as he brought himself under control. Two of the village women stumbled past, knocking into Dani in their haste. She stumbled to the side, but stayed upright. One of the women was crying and the other's eyes were wide in shock. A child wailed in the distance. Villagers were running in all directions, the panic evident.

"What happened?"

"Rebels from Sierra Leone are crossing the river. They're looking for the white doctors infecting the people."

"Oh, shit," Claire said. "How much time do we have?"

Travis bent over at the waist, with his hands on his hips, still breathing hard. "Not long. We have to leave. Now."

Everything inside was urging her to run. Panic was infectious, but she had to stay calm and rational. "We've dealt with this kind of superstition before."

"Yeah," Travis huffed. "But this patrol is rogue and

convinced we're the cause of this disease. And they aren't adverse to some ransom money either."

"They know we aren't protected?" Claire questioned.

He nodded, stood, and wiped his face with a red hankie. "I think they might be the ones who attacked the village forty miles from here. Retribution because we helped them as well."

"Damn it. We need more time." But she was realistic as well. If they really were bent on harming them, any villager in the way would be collateral damage. And Dani couldn't live with that.

"Pack up the essentials and leave everything else. We're out of here."

Claire spun back toward their office tent. "I'll get the laptops."

"I'll get Anuma and Hailey." Travis took off again. "We'll meet you back here and I'll bring the truck."

It was up to Dani to find Dr. Graham. A brilliant epidemiologist, he was also temperamental, and a complete tyrant about his work space. Which was why he had a tent to himself at the edge of the village.

Dani privately thought he was a narcissist with a God complex, but she was used to working with men like him. Her father was the same way.

"Martin?" she called, running toward his tent.

"Just a moment," he called from inside.

There was some rustling and it sounded as if something was slammed shut before the flap opened and Dr. Martin Graham stepped outside. His formerly starched white button down was rumpled, his perfectly pressed pants had lost their crispness, and Martin's hair had begun to go wild. He looked a bit like a mad scientist, but Dani stifled the urge to smile.

"Time to go, Martin."

He looked over his glasses at her, his gray eyes alert as he stared down at her. "What kind of trouble?"

"Rebels from Sierra Leone are on their way."

He waved his hand in the air—the movement impatient. "Things like this have happened before. Let the army deal with it."

"They would if they were here. But they aren't, remember? They left yesterday to deal with an attack on a neighboring village."

Martin took his glasses off and wiped the sweat off his face with his arm. "I can't leave yet."

Dani shook her head at him. "We have no choice. Pack what you can carry and be ready as soon as the truck pulls up." Then she started to turn away but added, "Five minutes, Martin. Or I'll have Travis and Anuma drag you out if I need to."

He might be the senior doctor, but she was team leader and would do what was necessary to ensure their survival. That's what she did. She saved lives. She'd lost too many people in her life and she wasn't losing anyone else. Even if it was a pain-in-the-ass doctor who expected everyone to bow down to his genius.

DAMON DUPREE PLAYED poker the same way he played women—with wild and reckless abandon. The fact that he was playing with three Marines and one very rich civilian only made the take sweeter. "Let's see 'em, boys."

And he laid his cards down. Straight flush—to the queen.

"Goddamn it, Shadow. How'd you pull that out?" The lance corporal threw his cards on the table. He'd had a full house. Kings over twos.

Not good enough.

The other two Marines didn't even bother showing their cards, just threw them on the table and pushed back to stand. Damon took all their cash, then looked at the only other civilian at the table. Dr. Gunner Halverson was a government asset sent to Africa because he was working on a cure for Ebola.

The doctor pushed his glasses up his nose and peered over his cards at Damon's straight flush. "Royal straight flush beats a regular straight flush, correct?"

Damon lost his grin. "Yep."

"Then you're one lucky bastard tonight," Gunner said, throwing down his pair of threes.

Damon blew out a breath and collected his winnings. "You had me worried for a second."

"I'm not sure you have the capability to worry about anything. Maybe I should stop playing poker with you and just empty out the cash in my pockets whenever you come around."

"That takes all the fun out of introducing you to new things," Damon said. The lance corporal and two Marines left the tent in disgust. Gunner and Damon were alone.

"I do new things all the time."

Damon grinned at Gunner's earnest face. "You never leave that mansion you own."

"We're in the middle of Liberia. How much more out of my house do you want me to be?"

"True. You get a pass for this one, but how long were you down in that invention room of yours?"

Gunner's eyebrows knit together. "It wasn't that long."

"You had a beard and looked malnourished."

"That's because George can't cook worth a damn."

"Well, then, fire him and hire someone who can."

Damon laughed as Gunner dropped his head into his hands, obscuring his face. "I never wanted a butler in the first place, but he sort of came with the house, so I can't fire him. I do have him order out quite a bit."

"He's old."

"Too old to find another job. Besides, he loves that house."

That Gunner referred to the monstrosity in Georgia as a house was amusing. Anything with ten bedrooms and twelve bathrooms, sitting on ten acres of land, should have its own classification. Damon wasn't sure old George even remembered there were three levels to the house. He'd never seen him attempt the stairs.

"Besides," Damon continued, "You were in that government 'think tank' for almost a year working on coming up with a cure for Ebola. You definitely lost a good thirty pounds that time. You looked pathetic."

"I was working round the clock," he said, frowning. "Lot of good that did everyone. They're not close enough and refuse to think outside the box."

"Well, that's why you left and started funding your own experiments to find a workable cure. With government sanction, even. That doesn't happen for everyone."

Lance Corporal Hicks stuck his head back inside the tent at that moment. "Call on the SAT phone for you."

Damon got up at once. "I made you eat something and take a break, so I guess you can go back to your lab now. See you tomorrow, Gunner. Bring more money."

"You're a fucking saint, Shadow."

Grinning at the finger he was being given and the scowl on Gunner's face, he turned and followed Hicks to the communications tent. They were stationed in a remote part of Liberia and the satellite phone was the only way to reach the outside world.

"Dupree."

"Good to hear your voice, son."

Damon felt his back straighten and something he didn't

want to name crawl through his guts. He knew that voice, even if he hadn't heard it for at least eight years. "Sir."

"I need your help, Damon. It's urgent," said Captain Nathanial Bordeaux.

Every time the Chief Scientist Officer of the U.S. Public Health Service called, Damon's life changed. Last time, it devastated him. But he was up for just about anything, which was why he was flying Gunner all over the world and into some of the worst hell-holes he'd ever seen. When he'd been discharged from the Marine Corps, he began to freelance his skills. Flying was one he enjoyed.

"What can I do for you, sir?"

"The CDC has a team in Guinea and they no longer have their government escort. Rebels are marching into the area and they're cut off from the other teams by the river. I need them flown out, son."

"You have some members of the Health Service there?"

"One, but I've worked with most of these people before, and I don't want to lose more doctors."

"How long do I have?"

"They evacuated the village, but the rebels will have them surrounded within the hour."

"I'm five hours away by air."

"Word is, this rebel leader from Sierra Leone is looking to make a name for himself by killing off anyone interfering in their culture. He's young and ignorant enough to believe that Western medicine is bad for them."

Damon dragged his palm down his face. Nathan's voice was thick with concern. A night extraction wasn't his favorite, but this was desperate. Desperate enough for Nathan to call him directly because he happened to be closer than anyone else.

"You have contact with them?"

"Some. I've got the coordinates of the location they're headed to for pickup."

Damon wrote them down. "I'm on it."

"Copy that. And, Damon?"

"Sir?"

"Watch out for Copperheads. I hear they're deadly."

Damon felt his whole body snap to attention. Damn, it had been a long time since he'd heard that code name. "I'll make it in three."

CHAPTER 2

*G*unfire erupted as Travis hit the gas. The truck bucked and threw Dani into Claire. Even Graham grimaced. The truck was a repurposed military transport vehicle and wasn't the smoothest ride.

"That was close," Travis said.

"We're not out of danger yet," Claire muttered. She looked at Dani. "Do you think the villagers made it out?"

Dani could feel the adrenaline in her system spiking her heart rate and making her take deep breaths. "I don't think they all left."

"But Travis warned the elders," Claire argued. Her face registered the horror they all felt.

All Dani could do was shake her head and pray they listened. So many of the villagers were too weak to move far. Having survived the Ebola virus, Dani was nauseous at the thought of misguided rebels now taking those lives. Her eyes met Martin's. His expression matched hers. There was nothing more anyone could do. It was no longer in their hands. Getting out of that village was the best way to save them. But the guilt by association was eating her up inside. It might not matter that they'd left; they still might punish the villagers for accepting help.

"Where are we going?" Claire asked.

"South toward the river. It's the flattest terrain I've seen to be able to land a plane or a chopper. Anuma agreed," Travis said.

"But that's toward Sierra Leone; isn't that too dangerous?"

Hailey Walsh had been quiet until that moment, eyes squeezed closed. But her voice had taken on a shrill tone that wobbled as she shook. Dani grabbed her hand and squeezed, pulling her focus and hoping to calm the woman. "It's too late to worry about it now. Travis and Anuma know what they're doing. Trust them."

Their normally silent guide, Anuma, reached back and patted Hailey as well. "It will be well." His accent was French, even through clenched teeth. He'd been the best guide they'd ever worked with and knew the country, as well as the social landscape of the villages.

He was from Ghana, but believed in Western medicine.

Then conversation stopped as the echoes of now distant gunfire reached their ears. Dani squeezed Hailey's hand harder. Even Graham's dour expression seemed more pronounced. Dani's world travels included time in the Peace Corps as well as the CDC, and she'd been in some fairly dangerous situations—this was worse than any of the other times.

This was the first time that she and her team were the specific targets.

"How many rebels, Travis?"

Dani could see the tendons in his neck standing out as he struggled to hold onto the wheel. They'd left the road and were blazing a path on the outskirts of the jungle. "At least twenty soldiers. But only one Jeep, so that is in our favor."

"Will they track us at night?" she asked.

It was Anuma who answered. "Yes. And we're leaving a trail big enough for a blind man to follow."

"It can't be helped, man," Travis said.

"What do you suggest, Anuma?" Dani asked.

Trekking through dense jungle at night wasn't just an unpleasant thought; it could be deadly. Night predators, snakes, and even insects would be teeming in the inky blackness. But against men with guns, the jungle *was* the only alternative. Even with all the evil bugs. She shuddered at the thought.

"We will have to leave the truck and hide in the trees."

She was afraid he was going to say that. "Can we put more distance between us first?"

Both he and Travis nodded. "We can hide the truck by the river and track backwards to the rendezvous spot."

"How long before they catch up with us?"

Travis shrugged. "Guess it depends on what happens in the village and how determined they are."

"I will hide us well," Anuma said.

Dani nodded. She believed he would try, but as she looked around at everyone in the truck, she knew it would be difficult. Four pale faces looked back. She knew her face echoed the terror they all felt. Her stomach was in knots and every bump threatened to release the panic she was carefully keeping in check. She was the leader and needed to keep calm.

But that didn't mean she couldn't worry about everything. Claire was in a stark white T-shirt that was a beacon in the light of the rising full moon. And Hailey's pale blonde hair would stand out like neon in the moonlight.

They were all in light colors, to stay cooler in the oppressive heat. But now those colors could alert the enemy to their location.

Only Anuma was in darker clothes, and with his obsidian hair and mocha skin, he would blend into the shadows flawlessly. He'd be able to disappear into safety on his own, but Dani was more than grateful that he was with them. And willing to help.

She reached out and laid her hand on his darker one. "Thank you, Anuma."

There was nothing more to say, no reassurance that she could give her team that they were going to make it out alive. There were no guarantees in this world. And they all knew it, even accepted it.

But that didn't mean she couldn't hope.

"I'm not actually sure a helicopter is supposed to make that kind of noise," Gunner said.

To his credit, his voice was steady and his posture was relaxed, but Damon wasn't fooled. Gunner was freaked out. Even with the headsets, they had to almost yell. "This baby will make it. Besides, I told you to stay at the base."

"But this is so much more exciting. I love flying," he said. "And maybe one of the lady doctors will think I'm handsome and heroic enough to reward me with a kiss, or a full night together."

Damon grinned. When Gunner wasn't lost in one of his inventions, he focused all his attention on women. All women. He loved everything about women and they loved him. Tall, blond, with deep brown eyes, he wasn't ever lacking in companions. Being rich and brilliant wasn't a bad asset either.

"What makes you think any of the docs are women?"

"Are you kidding? The CDC specializes in women who

want to make a difference in the world. Tough, but tender women, who aren't looking for a permanent man in their lives because they work for 'the cause'."

Damon checked his instrument panel with the coordinates he'd been given before he answered. "And you aren't a permanent kind of guy."

Gunner shrugged. "There are too many adventures and women in the world to settle down with only one. Besides, you're one to talk. When was the last time you had anything but a fling?"

Damon ignored that. It was true, but made him sound cold. "Well, you're in luck. There are three on this team. I'm sure at least one of them will be eternally grateful."

"Then hurry up and get there."

Damon handed Gunner a pair of night vision goggles. "We should be coming up to the clearing now. See if you can spot them."

"Got it."

He began to circle. No way was he landing if the team wasn't close. Gunner had been unable to reach the SAT phone the doctors were using, so he figured the battery must be dead or the phone damaged.

"Movement in the trees. Four—no, six bodies."

Then they both saw the bright red of a flare spring to life. Damon saw the tip moving and then another one was lit. Both bounced along as they were carried to the clearing. He circled the open space as more flares were lit and placed on the ground, illuminating his landing area.

"Shit. Land now," Gunner said. He pointed toward the river. Headlights jumped up and down in the distance. "That's muzzle flash. They're shooting at us."

"Copy that."

Damon pushed the stick down and used his pedals to

make the landing as smooth as possible, but going down that fast made his stomach drop. The blades above them whined at the abrupt movement, then they settled down into the normal thump, thump noise they usually made. He set them down with a hard thud. Gunner was cussing steadily under his breath, so Damon was only catching every other word. He made sure his door faced the headlights angling toward them.

"Get everyone inside, Gun."

He heard Gunner acknowledge him as he moved. His M-40A3 sniper rifle felt comfortable in his hands. Flying was the second best thing he did; killing was the first. He'd been one of the best Marine snipers in the Corps. And it was time to slow down the rebels. He couldn't see anyone in the pitch black, but they couldn't drive fast without headlights. Those, he could see. And if he happened to wing a couple, then so be it.

When he had a rifle in his hands, he didn't miss.

DANI HAD Claire and Hailey by the hands as one of the pilots jumped out of the chopper and slid open the door to the passenger area. It looked like a Vietnam era Huey, minus the gun turrets. And it wasn't until she was almost inside that she saw the name scrawled on the side.

Archangel.

That's when she stumbled.

Dani hadn't thought about who was coming for them; she assumed it would be someone from the military. She never dreamed it would be a civilian. She never dreamed it would be him.

Damon Dupree.

15

"Oh, God, the rebels," Claire yelled over the noise of the copter blades. Dani saw the headlights in the distance, just as one went black and the noise of a large caliber weapon sounded from the other side of the helicopter.

"Everyone in, now," yelled the big man waving them over.

Gunfire erupted in the distance as the second headlight was extinguished suddenly. Everyone was running, but the wind from the rotating blades pushed against them. Hurry, hurry, her mind screamed. She wasn't about to get inside until her whole team was safe, but it was a battle against the adrenaline surging through her, demanding she jump inside and be done with it. Once everyone had climbed in, she threw herself inside as the door was sliding closed. Both the pilots jumped back into the front and they were up off the ground in a move that caused everyone to give a startled gasp.

Damon didn't have a single light on inside or out, probably to make them an impossible target. With no lights, the rebels could only guess at their location in the sky by the sound. And they were moving so fast, Dani was sure they were out of range. Her breathing was so ragged that she had to lean forward, elbows on knees to catch a breath. While it was still loud inside, she was able to pick out other noises, such as Hailey's crying. Everyone else was in the same condition Dani was, breathing fast, but trying to get it under control.

Small lights flickered to life in the back after a while. There was only enough light to see everyone's relieved faces. The big man in the co-pilot chair turned and grinned at them and gave them a thumb's up. Then, he pointed above their heads.

Dani reached up, already knowing what was there. Headsets. Slipping hers over her ears, she helped Claire with hers and showed the rest of them the switch they could hit to talk.

"Is everyone okay back there?"

His voice made her want to cry, but also sounded so sweet in her ears that she couldn't speak past the fist-sized lump in her throat. It had been at least eight years since she'd seen Damon in person.

"We're all alive, thanks to you two," Travis said.

The rest of her crew added their thanks, but Dani hadn't said anything. She couldn't yet. It was amazing that after all these years the sound of his voice had this effect on her. Her chest was tight and she had to close her eyes and count before she could calm down. It was as if the years had fallen away and she'd been given a precious glimpse into the past.

"How're you holding up, Red?"

That made her eyes fly open, only to meet five very curious pairs. Good thing it was too dark to see the blush making its way up her neck and into her cheeks. No one dared call her that, and her team was waiting for the rare explosion that normally happened when someone did.

"As well as can be expected, Shadow." She ducked her head to hide her grin. "How'd you get mixed up in this?"

"I heard there was a Copperhead sighting and happened to be in the area."

That earned him a tired chuckle and some incredulous looks from everyone else. Dani's team had never seen her act this way with anyone but themselves. And they'd only managed to loosen up her tight reserve after being with her for several years.

"It figures. Dad never does let me go completely off the radar."

"Of course not, the last time he did you created an international incident."

"I did not start that one, and you know it. That was all...," she trailed off.

"Yeah, it was," Damon finished for her and she could hear

the distant echoes of the pain she carried with her in his voice. "Aren't you going to introduce me to your friends?"

Dani looked around at her team, who were exchanging confused looks. "Everyone, this is Damon Dupree. My brother-in-law."

CHAPTER 3

The temporary military base in Liberia had a tent with hot showers. Real hot water that rained down onto her head. It was a little bit of heaven for Dani, but due to the adrenaline dump, tears that were hotter than the water streamed down her face. Slow sobs bubbled up and escaped as she stood under the hot spray. Since she was alone, she let herself have a good cry. It was raw and ugly, but she didn't care.

They could have died. All of them.

It took a bit, but her muscles began to unknot as the terror seeped from her body. It wasn't as easy to wipe away as the soap, but she was under control again.

Dani made her way back to the tent assigned to her, thinking she still had an angel sitting on her shoulder. Gabriel. It had been a long time since she felt his presence, and even though she wasn't a religious person, she believed in angels. He'd always been hers, even more so after he'd died and left her.

Obviously, his twin brother carried Gabriel with him as

well. He'd even named his helicopter after his brother. *Archangel.* It warmed her heart to see the nickname.

And then suddenly he was there. The shadow to his twin's bright light. *Damon.* Long wavy black hair with eyes the color of topaz. So achingly familiar and yet—not.

"Come here," he said.

And she flew into his arms, wrapping herself in his muscular embrace. "Thank you for coming for us."

"As if there were any other option."

Dani broke their quick embrace and moved away before she did something stupid, like cry all over him. And just when she had gotten herself under control. It was just—well —so damned wonderful to be in his arms because for one infinitesimal moment, it was like Gabriel was back and holding her.

And she couldn't use Damon that way. It wasn't right.

"Why are you even here in Liberia?" she asked.

Damon shrugged. "Babysitting on Uncle Sam's dime."

"I heard you'd gone into business for yourself. Although, mercenary is an ugly word."

He laughed and said, "That sounds like something your father would say."

Dani sat on her cot with her legs crossed in front of her as she began to comb out the tangles in her long red hair. "Well, yeah, he's the one I heard it from."

Damon made himself comfortable in the chair by her makeshift desk. He looked older than she remembered, but then it had been at Gabriel's funeral that she'd seen him last. And that had been through a haze of pain so intense that she'd blocked out most of that entire year.

He was leaner, harder somehow, than he'd been in the Marines. And even more handsome than the last time she'd seen him.

"Why are you still crusading, Dani? You should be in a private hospital, stateside, working normal hours."

She ducked her head, not knowing how to answer him, because for the last couple of years, she'd been asking herself the same thing. But this was the only life she'd known, and it was hard to give up the familiarity, even comfort of it. "How could I give all this up?"

The smile that slowly emerged as he looked around the sparse tent made her stomach clench.

"True. World travel, danger, and no regard for personal hygiene. Now, that's the life."

"How about you? Why aren't you married with five kids?"

That got a raised eyebrow from him. "What makes you think I'm not?"

Dani shook her head. "No woman in her right mind would let you continue being a Merc if you had five mouths to feed. It's not exactly the most stable job. Or the safest."

"Let's just say that I've never found anyone who measures up."

Instantly, an image of the one and only kiss they'd ever shared sprang to mind. It was the night she'd gotten engaged to Gabriel, and Damon happened to be home on leave. She'd had a bit too much to drink and made a mistake. An honest one, but embarrassing as well, because she'd never before had trouble telling them apart, but only because their hair was so differently styled. Everything else was startlingly similar, especially since she'd never had any experience with identical twins.

It wasn't until she tried to bury her fingers in his hair that the shock of his buzz cut jerked her into reality. Gabriel's hair was longer, softer, and his kiss had never been quite that wild. As if he were trying to eat her alive. Damon's kiss had scared her.

"What are you thinking about?" he asked, when the silence had gone on a moment too long.

Dani could barely meet his eyes and was very much afraid that she blushed. "I'm sorry, I got lost in thought. What were we talking about?"

He didn't believe her, she could tell, but he changed the subject anyway.

"My orders were to get you back to this base safely. What are you and your team doing next?"

"We were only two days from being deployed back home, but I wasn't prepared to go just yet."

He cocked his head to the side and stared at her. What he saw she wasn't sure, but it startled her when he asked, "What did you find?"

Because he'd always been able to read her like that. Even Gabriel couldn't do that, and it had always made her uneasy. "How do you do that?"

"I play a lot of poker, Red. I can spot a 'tell' immediately."

"What gave me away?"

He grinned and shook his head. "If I let you know, then I wouldn't have that ace anymore. So, what's going on in that pretty head of yours that would prevent you from leaving?"

She sighed. Dani hadn't confided in anyone, because she wasn't sure of her findings. Not yet. And the last of her samples were left behind in that village. She had to get back there.

It would be nice to tell someone her fears. And Damon could be trusted.

"I think someone is altering the Ebola strain," she finally said.

He didn't question her or show any disbelief, which a statement like that might cause with anyone else. She could have hugged him for that. "Altering it how?"

"Shortening its incubation period and making it stronger."

"Shit."

"Exactly."

"How did you find out?"

Dani threw the brush she'd been using on her hair down on the cot and moved toward her desk. Her personal journal was in her bag sitting on top. "We take samples of blood from everyone infected, and when we got to the village, we found exactly what we expected to. But then, one of the women, who'd seemed fine, suddenly had symptoms. And it progressed at a faster pace than it should have. Not only that, but we couldn't trace where the strain came from."

"That's unusual?" he asked.

Finding the journal, she opened to the page where she'd sketched out the virus. It always reminded her of a backwards J with fancy swirls on top. She pointed to the normal virus. "This is what we see in almost one hundred percent of infection cases."

Then she pointed at a second picture that was nearly identical with the exception of three lines that looked like hairs jutting off of the main body of the virus. "Do you see these?"

"It's almost unnoticeable."

"Exactly. And when we found the villager that we thought was patient zero, this was what the sample looked like."

Damon looked up at her. "But?"

"But," she leaned down next to him. "This wasn't patient zero. And this woman died five days after we landed in that village."

"So, what are you thinking?"

Dani could feel the horror creeping into her tone, something she'd lived with for the past month. "That someone on my team is altering this virus and killed several people in that village as a trial run. And, now, I don't have any proof because my samples disappeared not long after those rebels attacked."

"A trial run for something bigger. Maybe an attack on a larger, more important target?"

"I don't know."

DAMON LEANED back in his chair. The mild soap mixed with Dani's unique fragrance filled his senses and he tended to lose perspective when she was close. And what she told him needed laser focus.

"How can you be sure it's someone on your team?"

"I can't be completely sure, but I have a feeling. Add that to the fact that we were the only team in that area, and it doesn't make sense for it to be anyone else. And it pisses me off because I trusted everyone on my team."

"How are they altering the virus?"

She sighed and rubbed her forehead. Damon could see the strain around her eyes. This was taking its toll on her.

"I don't know. The only thing I can think is that it was manufactured in a lab, and then transported with us to the village. We just don't have that kind of equipment available when we're sent in." Dani paced the length of the tent. "I just don't understand why."

Damon could answer that one. "It's usually money."

"But we take an oath to help people, to cure the world of its diseases. How could someone I work with do something like this?"

"And how many of you have big Tudor houses with fancy sports cars and large investment portfolios?"

Dani swung her head in his direction. "More than you'd think."

He shrugged. Dani, and even his brother Gabriel, both had their heads in an idealistic cloud. Always had. "Money is power, Red. And if that isn't the goal, then I would have to assume that one of your good doctors has a God complex."

She sat down abruptly on the cot where she'd been brushing her hair and put her head in her hands. "I don't have proof of any of this."

"Could the virus have mutated on its own?"

Damon watched as she bit her lower lip and his body responded, but he ruthlessly pushed it down. His iron will had served him well in the past and he counted on it now to keep his mind on the present and potential threat, and not her full lower lip. Or her copper colored hair beginning to dry and curl in the humidity.

Dani shook her head. "Not this fast. Viruses mutate all the time, but it happens slowly. This was definitely lab grown."

"So, who is your primary suspect?"

"I have a doctor on my team with that God complex you were talking about, but I've worked with him for years. Why now? And as for the rest of my team, I just can't wrap my head around any of them deliberately causing the death of anyone, much less almost an entire village."

"Sounds like we need to get you that proof."

"Even with the blood samples, it still doesn't tell me who it is."

Damon smiled. "Once those samples come to light, I'm sure the government will take over the investigation."

"And cover everything up, nice and neat. Problem solved. No need for anyone to know about it."

"True. This could be a huge black eye for more than one agency, but it would stop mass murder, even if it never goes public."

"How can you be so...so cavalier about it?"

"I've worked for the government most of my adult life

and there are some things out in the big bad scary world that the general public is better off not knowing."

Damon knew he was right, but he could see the determination in those leaf green eyes. The crusader was there, looking back at him in defiance. And he knew he wasn't going to be able to resist her when she asked for his help. She would, eventually. And when she stirred up the shit storm, he'd be there to protect her.

Because he owed it to his brother. At least, that's what he told himself.

CHAPTER 4

"So, that's your brother's wife," Gunner drawled, never taking his eyes from the cards he held. A half-eaten sandwich sat next to him at the table.

The question was there, but Damon wasn't sure how to answer it. And he couldn't stop from looking up as Dani crossed the compound to the medical tent. Her bright hair was braided, hanging long down her back. Plain white T-shirt and khaki shorts that cupped her perfect ass completed the ensemble. More than one soldier stopped to stare as she passed, but she was oblivious to the frank appreciation.

"His widow," he muttered, before turning back to his own hand of cards. She looked good this morning, like she'd gotten some sleep. "Finish your food, Gunner."

"Call," he said. A certain amount of triumph was in his voice.

Damon glanced outside the tent again. "Fold."

"That's it, I quit."

Dragging his attention back to his friend, Damon raised an eyebrow. "You won." It was with some surprise that he realized that he hadn't really noticed. And he'd just thrown away a flush.

Gunner made a disgusted noise. "I've won the last five hands, not that you'd remember. Your concentration is for shit. Something else on your mind besides my eating habits?"

"Leave the cards and let's get out of here."

Once they'd left the tent and had some privacy, Damon laid out Dani's suspicions. Gunner was brilliant in many ways, but one of his degrees was in biochemical engineering. He wanted Gunner's opinion about the situation.

"So, she thinks one of her people has cooked up a faster more vicious strain?"

Damon nodded. "Says she had some samples back in that camp, but they were left behind in their rush to get out of the village before the rebels attacked."

"You think it's a coincidence those soldiers attacked that camp when they did?"

"I don't like coincidence. In my experience, most things happen for a reason."

Gunner agreed as they started walking again. "What we'd need is to find is the money trail. Someone is getting paid to mutate that virus. It usually comes down to greed."

"Unless we have a psychopath on our hands," Damon said. "I'll tap some resources in the states to start doing some digging into Dani's team, but I want you looking at those samples with Dani. If we can recover them."

"No need to ask. I want those samples. And if what the lady suspects is true, then I'm going to want someone's ass."

That's what he thought Gunner might say. He was a crusader as well, in his own way. But his curiosity and sense of righteousness were going to get him into some serious trouble one day when Damon wasn't around to protect his back. "I'll work on getting back into that village."

"Is your redhead going?"

The thought of Dani back in potential danger made something ugly swirl around his gut, but he didn't have the right to stop her. He could try and talk her out of it, but knew she'd be stubborn and he needed her to guide them to the right place. So he merely said, "Most likely."

Gunner grinned and Damon thought he must have sounded as disgruntled as he felt. He couldn't seem to hold onto his poker face when he thought about her. Which was why he'd stayed away so long and kept himself busy.

"I think I'll make some calls and then see if I can find that cute little blonde doctor. Claire isn't it? Or was it Hailey?" Gunner wiggled his eyebrows and turned to go.

"Claire has the auburn hair, Hailey is the blonde. Both are good looking and have that caring look you're so fond of. Have fun," Damon called after him.

"Always."

DANI FELT RESTED after that crazy night and ready to get back to work when she entered the medical tent. At the very least, she could help out with inoculations. The locals had begun bringing their sick into camp. No Ebola cases, but this was a base camp in Liberia. A starting point from which the CDC and the military would fan out to begin checking the villages.

"What are you doing up?" Claire said, walking over and taking off her latex gloves with a pop.

"Thought I'd come over and help out for a while. Besides, I'm going blind from paperwork."

Claire made a face. "All the shots have been given already, but I understand getting away from those damn reports. I mean, how many different ways can you describe one thing?"

"How about next time you get to be team leader?" Dani smiled.

A shudder racked Claire's body. "And be responsible for everyone *and* all the paperwork? No thanks."

Dani watched Claire as she began cataloguing medical supplies to help the primary team that had arrived with the military unit. Setting up was always a tedious endeavor and Claire was always the first to jump in to help. Dani was having a hard time imagining her friend doing anything as nefarious as mutating a virus to kill innocent people.

But then, no one on her team seemed likely.

And it was possible that she'd made a mistake. The conditions were bad, and while the supplies they had were top notch, they weren't the state-of-the-art machines and equipment they had back in Atlanta. It would be so easy to blame exhaustion and an epidemic for her sudden paranoia. But ever since the attack by the Sierra Leone rebels, Dani felt hunted. As if she were being watched all the time, and it was a feeling she couldn't shake.

"Where's Hailey this morning?"

Claire looked around. "She was here about an hour ago helping with the shots, but I got busy and lost track of her." She shrugged. "You know how she is. There is an entire base of hot guys here."

"And Hailey would relish the adulation she is undoubtedly receiving." Looking around, Dani noticed that the rest of the doctors and staff were out of earshot. "What is everyone else up to today?"

Claire rolled her eyes. "Well, Martin, I mean, *Doctor Graham*," she dragged out his name sarcastically, "Came in and tried to take over like the Lord of the Manor. But that wiry little guy over there shut him down. So he left."

Glancing toward the other side of the makeshift hospital, Dani saw the little guy in question. She'd met him last night and knew his name was Dr. Montgomery (call me Monty) Nelson. A nice guy with wire-rimmed glasses, bright blue eyes, and a no nonsense attitude about medicine. That he'd stood up to Dr. Graham's naturally autocratic nature made him go up in Dani's already high opinion of the man.

"Good for Monty."

"I don't normally go for smaller guys, but watching him shut down Martin was kinda sexy."

Dani noticed that Claire had a considering look on her face as she looked around and found him.

"But, really, that friend of Damon's, what's his name?"

Dani smiled, "Gunner."

"Now, him, I wouldn't mind taking into the shower to do dirty things with." Then she sighed and went back to cataloguing supplies. "If Hailey hasn't sunk her claws into him yet, that is."

"Have you noticed anyone acting strangely on this trip?" Dani tried to sound casual, and she was taking a risk by asking Claire, but damn it, she knew her. Inside and out. And she considered her a very good friend. Her only real friend these days.

Claire swung her head around and narrowed her eyes. "Strange how?"

"I don't know," Dani shook her head. "Maybe it's just me, but this trip has just been different. I wondered if you'd noticed it too." *And please don't be the one doing this horrible thing.*

Claire bit her lip and looked around to make sure they were still relatively alone. "Now that you mention it, I'm worried about Travis."

That took her by surprise. "Why?"

"Well, he's been less talkative than usual and he stayed gone from the last village too long, you know? I mean, sometimes he takes longer to track down relatives, but he was tense the whole time and kept just disappearing without telling anyone. And we all know that's just dangerous."

Dani hadn't realized. She'd been so busy trying to contain the outbreak that she'd been putting in more hours than the rest of the team. But that was normal for her. What Claire was describing definitely wasn't normal Travis behavior.

"Maybe he'd talk to you," she said. "I bet you can find out if everything is okay."

"Well, I can try, but he's always seemed a bit more comfortable with Hailey." Dani had wondered from time to time of they were lovers, but had never seen any evidence of it. "I wonder why they never dated. Back in the states, I mean."

Claire threw her head back and laughed. "You can be so clueless sometimes."

"What am I missing?"

"He's half in love with you, idiot."

That took Dani off guard. "What? You can't be serious."

"I can't believe you haven't noticed. He hangs on your every word and follows you around carrying all your stuff."

"But he does that with everyone. He's always been nice and helpful." *How could she have not noticed a crush?* "Damn," Dani muttered. "I almost wish you hadn't told me."

Claire reached out and put her hand on Dani's shoulder, giving a commiserating look. "Not your fault. He knows you haven't let go of Gabriel yet. We all know you still love him."

Was that it? Or was there something else going on with Travis? Dani tried to hide the quick wince at Claire's matter of fact words. Eight years was a long time to mourn a dead husband. Is that what they all thought? That she hadn't moved on?

Had she moved on?

Maybe she hadn't or maybe she'd just been so focused on saving lives that she hadn't realized how alone she'd become.

32

Not even noticing a younger man's admiration. But she had moved on…she really thought she had. Otherwise she wouldn't be having such a strong reaction to Damon.

But that wasn't important. Finding out who was responsible for mutating an already deadly virus was her priority. Not going and finding Damon and listening to his deep voice, or staring into light brown eyes that reminded her of a tiger.

Or having him take her in his arms. She suppressed a mild shudder.

Or more.

CHAPTER 5

*W*hen the line picked up, it sounded like the play area in the mall. It was so loud that Damon pulled the phone away from his ear to recheck the number.

Then a disgruntled voice bellowed, "Yeah?"

"Mike?"

"What?"

Damon stifled a laugh as it became obvious that Mike was surrounded by children. Several of which were crying. "It's Damon. You need some backup?"

"You have no idea. Hold on, will ya?"

Before Damon could say anything, he heard Mike in the background. "Damn it, Xavier, stop cutting the Barbie doll's hair; you know that's not your toy. Jessica, stop crying. Yes, I'm sure your daddy will get you another one." Then there was rustling and the crying became loud sniffles.

"Here, talk to Uncle Damon."

It was everything Damon could do not to laugh out loud at the chaos he was hearing. His friend was clearly babysitting. 'Little' Mike Hansen had been one of the toughest Marines in the Corps along with his two buddies, Zach Steele and Jesse Calhoun. And when Zach and Jesse had each settled down and had kids, he'd become the wimpiest babysitter Damon had ever seen. Those kids had Mike wrapped around their little fingers. It was pathetic.

"Hi, Uncle Damon."

"Are you causing trouble, Xavier?" He put his best Uncle voice on.

"I didn't do it; I swear. It was Jennifer this time, honest." Xavier Steele was five years old and a little demon. A cute one to be sure, but a hellion just like his father was at that age, or so Zach claimed. Damon had never personally witnessed the big man doing anything that wasn't calm and methodical, but then, Zach tended to be a bit unpredictable these days.

The two girls sniffling in the background were Jennifer and Jessica Calhoun. Four year old identical twins, and just as mischievous as their "cousin." Jesse had his hands full with those two. Damon couldn't even tell them apart, and that was sad, considering he'd been a twin himself.

"What's your job as the oldest?"

A long drawn out sigh crackled through the SAT phone. "I protect the twins and be a good role model."

Damon grinned. "And are you doing that?"

Again the sigh. "I could do better." It was clearly an answer drummed into him since it was said with such dramatic flair.

"Okay, buddy, work on it and put Uncle Mike back on the phone, okay?"

"Okay. Bye, Uncle Damon."

The TV flared to life in the background, and suddenly the cacophony of tears stopped and it was quiet, with the exception of a song about a pineapple under the sea. "I should have done that earlier," Mike said.

"I think you're outflanked."

"Hell, I *know* I am." There was a pause. "So what can I do for you, Shadow? Last I heard, you were babysitting Gunner overseas."

"I need some intel on five targets."

"What's up?"

Damon rubbed the back of his neck as he stared down into the camp. Soldiers moved with purpose, either doing drills or finishing setting up. He was up a tall hill to make sure he was not overheard. And down below, one Dr. Martin Graham was acting very strange for someone with nothing to hide.

He wished he had the scope from his rifle; he would've been able to see expressions clearly from this range with it. He watched the good doctor while saying, "Someone with the CDC might be mutating the Ebola virus to make it stronger and faster."

"I don't like the sound of that," Mike's voice lowered. "Give me the names."

After Damon rattled of the names and dates of birth, he asked, "You still have those contacts from your time in Intelligence?"

"Yep. I'll find out what I can."

"Thanks, man. I owe you."

Mike sighed. "One day, I'm calling in all these favors."

Damon grinned. "And when you do, I'm sure it'll be epic."

"Semper Fi!"

That's when the doctor slipped into Dani's tent. And Damon started down the hill.

~

"WHAT THE HELL are you doing here, Martin?"

The doctor flinched, his only reaction to being caught in Dani's tent uninvited. Then he straightened away from her desk, where he'd been looking through some of her notes, and shoved his hands in his pockets.

"I was waiting for you, of course," he said, sounding bored.

Dani moved further into the space toward her desk, forcing Martin to move aside. Her notes were undisturbed and were part of the report that would be submitted to the CDC upon return to the states. Nothing of her suspicions went into this report, so there was no reason for her to be upset with finding one of her team members waiting.

But she was.

"Next time, please come find me instead of snooping through my personal notes."

Making a noise that sounded a bit like an indignant huff, Martin responded, "I was merely curious while waiting. Besides, if there was something in the report that wasn't meant for other's consumption then it shouldn't be left strewn about for anyone to see."

She buried the irritation somewhat as Dani reluctantly agreed. But she'd be damned if she let the walking thesaurus know it. Instead, she sat down at her desk and pointed to the cot, motioning him to sit. Not that he would. "I assume your reports are ready as well? As soon as a transport is ready, then we're headed stateside."

"Of course," he said, never giving the cot a glance.

Martin chose the high ground, preferring to stand, towering over the now sitting Dani. It didn't bother her. Dr. Martin Graham liked the illusion of being in charge, always, and she'd learned to deal with it. And giving him what he perceived as an advantage was easier than fighting him for it.

"So, why are you in here?"

"I heard you were going back to the village."

How he'd heard, she had no idea. She didn't deny it. "We're leaving soon."

"I'll be going with you," he said. "I want the rest of my equipment from my tent in the village."

"You weren't invited." She said it calmly and waited for the tirade. Not that Martin was the yelling type, more the throw-his-authority-around type. But, in this instance, he wasn't going to win the argument.

"You may be team leader on this trip, but I do outrank you. I will be going."

"Doesn't matter who you think you are, Doc. Like the lady said, you weren't invited."

Damon's voice was calm and smooth, but the edge was unmistakable. Dani slumped back into her seat and let Martin have a taste of real authority. The kind that didn't respond to titles or even societal standards—and especially rudely stated demands.

But Martin tried anyway. "As the senior doctor, I should be present to collect the rest of the data that was unavoidably left behind."

Damon shrugged. His olive green T-shirt was plastered to his muscled chest from the heat, outlining a form that was ripped and cut. Camouflage BDU pants hugged lean hips and strong thighs. About an inch under six feet tall, he was every-thing Martin's pressed perfection would never be...naturally confident and physically imposing.

Dani was amused to see the superiority of one ex-Marine slowly deflate Martin's ego. At least he knew when he was outmatched. He was certainly outgunned, since Damon also happened to be armed and his hand rested lightly on his holstered weapon.

"Everything alright here, Dani?"

"It's fine. Really. Dr. Graham was leaving and I just wanted to grab my backpack before we headed out."

"Well, then, how about I escort the good Doc back to his quarters and meet you at the helipad in five?"

Snapping a smart salute from her chair, Dani smiled and said, "Copy that, Marine."

Damon's grin sent an unexpected stab right through her. So like Gabriel's and yet, all his own. He was the reckless twin, the one prone to starting trouble, just to see how everyone reacted. He'd always been that way, while his brother had been cautious, exploring all the options and making the informed decision.

"I demand to go along."

Martin had his arms crossed and a pugnacious look on his face. She sighed. Soothing his bruised ego wasn't on her agenda and she didn't have time for it. Other things demanded her attention before they left. "Look, Martin..."

"Time to go, Doc," Damon said, grabbed Martin by the shoulders, and shoved him toward the tent opening. "Let me help you out."

Dani hadn't realized that he'd already moved around behind Dr. Graham. "Take your hands off of me." His voice was higher than normal in surprise at being stiff-leg walked out into the compound.

"Sorry about this Doc, really, but the lady has more important things to do than deal with your bullshit."

That Damon actually sounded like he cared made Dani bite her lower lip to keep the laughter at bay. It was really nice to have someone else take charge for once. It had been a long time since she'd had that particular luxury.

And when Damon's head popped back into the tent, she couldn't stop the grin. "That was mean."

He shrugged and grinned back. "Move your ass, Red. We have a time-table."

"Yes, sir."

He was gone and she jumped up to empty her trusty backpack. Those samples were going to stay with her at all times once she had them back. Damon's friend, Gunner, wanted to look them over and Dani welcomed the new set of eyes. Maybe she was tired and overworked. Maybe she just imagined the mutation.

And maybe she really did have a killer on her team. She was hoping Gunner would be able to spot the truth. For the first time in her life, Dani wanted to be wrong.

HAILEY STOPPED NEXT to Travis under the overhang of the mess tent. From where they stood, they had a great view of Dani's tent and everything that was going on outside of it. Which included that helicopter pilot and Dr. Graham in a short, but heated argument.

"What's going on over there?" she asked.

"I'm not sure," Travis said, "but I don't like the way that guy just barged into Dani's tent."

"As opposed to Dr. Graham barging into her tent?"

Travis shrugged, and they both watched as Dr. Graham straightened his clothes and walked away, fists clenched and sour expression on his face. "Yeah, but he's always doing something like that. We don't know this guy."

Hailey rolled her eyes. "He's her brother-in-law, so I'm sure it's fine, Trav."

That guy stuck his head back into the tent and then took off toward the far edge of camp, where his helicopter was sitting. She hadn't realized Travis was tense until he relaxed his shoulders and flexed his back.

"What would you have done anyway?" she asked, honestly curious. "That guy would've taken you apart."

Travis snorted. "I can handle myself."

Hailey reached out to touch his arm, the rare contact making her fingers tingle. Too bad he never noticed. He never noticed anything—or anyone—when Dani was around. She was like a magnet, pulling him closer without ever really letting him as close as he so obviously wanted to be.

Look at me, she thought. *I'm right here.* But she never said anything. She knew a lost cause when she saw one, and she also knew that Dr. Danielle Bordeaux was completely oblivious to Travis's obsession.

But she wasn't oblivious to that pilot. That was for sure. Her whole body language changed when she was with him. Too bad Travis couldn't see that. Or maybe he didn't want to.

"I should go and check on her. Make sure she doesn't need anything."

Hailey tightened her grip, finally earning a quick look from him. "Maybe you should let her be. She's a big girl and clearly has some history with Damon."

Travis shrugged her off about the time Dani left the tent and turned to head in the direction that Damon had taken a few minutes earlier. "You don't understand, Hailey. She doesn't understand either, but I do. I found out all about that guy from some of the other soldiers here."

She sighed and shoved her hands into the pockets of her khaki pants. "What don't I understand?"

"He's a killer. Some kind of ex-Marine sniper turned mercenary. I'll bet Dani doesn't know about that, and someone should tell her to stay away from him. He's not good for her."

And you are? Instead, she said, "And what do you hope to gain by telling her all that?"

Travis frowned down at her, "You don't understand." And he stepped away from Hailey to follow Dani.

"Oh, I think I understand just fine," she whispered. "You're the one that doesn't understand."

But he would. And eventually he'd turn to her.

At least, a girl could hope.

CHAPTER 6

*D*amon pulled the stick back and the chopper left the ground as another member of Dani's team rounded the corner. That one was named Travis and he had a determined look on his face. But they didn't have time for more delays and Dani wouldn't have been able to see him as they flew off. Damon made sure.

"How long is the flight?" Dani asked from the seat next to him.

He thought she looked hot all strapped in with her headset on and Gunner's aviation glasses shielding her vivid eyes from the sun—and him.

"Five hours, give or take."

"I hope it's worth the trip. Especially for those guys in the back."

Damon glanced back at the five volunteers. The lance corporal that he'd fleeced in poker was among them. "Don't let them fool you. They were bored as hell and looking for something to do."

"But deliberately flying into a possibly dangerous situation for some medical supplies and my slides isn't something they'd normally do for fun. Even if they are Marines. And how did you get it approved in the first place?"

"You mean because I'm just a lowly mercenary now with no military ranking?"

He grinned when she shot him the bird, and then again when she immediately checked to make sure no one caught her doing something so un-doctorly. "That's not what I said."

"You didn't have to. Everyone gets their orders, and it so happens that one of my orders is to provide one Dr. Gunner Halverson whatever he needs in terms of resources for his experiments. He decided he needed your slides." He winked at her and then went back to watching the instrument panel. "And the corporal back there saw you, just so you know."

"They can't hear us, right?"

He laughed. "Nope. Are you going cuss me out now?"

Her laugh rumbled low through the headset. She needed to laugh more often. She'd been such a serious little thing when Gabriel had brought her home to Louisiana during college. They'd just joined the Peace Corps after earning their degrees. Damon had been home for some R&R after Bagdad and was enjoying some of his mama's home cooking and his daddy's raunchy sense of humor.

As if she'd known his train of thought, she asked seriously, "How's your dad?"

"Probably illegally poaching gators again, now that Mama passed and can't forbid it."

"I'm sorry about that. I should have gone to the funeral."

He shrugged, "He got your card. Still sitting on his side table, last I was there." Damon didn't want to guilt her into spending time with the old man, but his Dad loved her as the daughter he didn't have. "He'd love it if you went home to visit."

"I haven't been able to face him."

Something in her voice was so sad that it almost broke his

heart. "Why not? He loves you to pieces, even if you didn't keep the Dupree name."

"Because I couldn't save him, Damon." It came out a choked whisper. "I'm a doctor and I failed. I didn't save Gabriel."

ANUMA ABENAA WAS HIDING in the jungle, watching as the rebel soldiers led away the last of the villagers. The ones they'd left alive. He'd slipped away from the military camp the night before. Almost the moment they'd landed, he'd gotten lost in the crowd and made his way to the nearest village. He'd stolen a beat up truck to make this trip. He doubted he'd be missed until today, and by then, he'd have done what he came to do.

Which was to destroy evidence.

Everyone had something to hide, and he was no different. Eventually, he'd be found out, but for the time being, he was content to lead a life where everyone thought they knew him. It suited him, to work with the CDC as a translator. And if he was less than honest about some of his translations, it couldn't be helped.

After the rebels did their final sweep, the village was empty. And still he waited at least thirty minutes before leaving the cover of the dense jungle. There was no one to witness it as he crept forward, darting into the tents to grab items he knew to be valuable. Still, he was careful, keeping to the waning shadows as the sun started to go down. And when he had what he wanted, he wrapped some cloth around a long stick and lit it on fire.

This can't be helped, he told himself. The village elders would rebuild, like they always did when tragedy struck. Anuma began to set the tents on fire, the embers flying high.

That was when he heard the unmistakable thump, thump of the helicopter blades.

The chopper came in fast and low and was the same one from their rescue. He stood frozen, flaming torch still in hand as it passed by. The glare of the sun obscured his vision of the pilot and co-pilot, but the five men with guns in the back were pretty clear.

He dropped the torch and ran, the satchel around his back bouncing with every movement.

How did they know? It was too soon. He couldn't get caught yet.

Not yet.

~

"Was that—?"

Dani's hands gripped the belt strapping her in as she leaned as close to the window as she could. Her face was almost pressed against the glass. "Anuma? Yes, it was," she answered.

Damon swung them around and turned toward the now burning village. "What the hell is he doing here?"

"Good question. But I want to know why he's burning the village down. Can we land?"

"Yeah, I saw a flat spot close by."

When they landed, the five Marines in the back jumped out with weapons ready. They fanned out and took point, while Dani followed. Damon stayed close, one hand resting lightly on her back and the other holding his gun. He was protecting their backsides.

"What do you know about your guide?"

Dani shook her head. "Not much when I really think about it. He was cleared through the CDC and the local

46

government and he's been on several assignments with different teams in Ghana."

"What about personally? Where's he from?"

The heat of the fire was reaching them, heating Dani's face and making them all sweat. "He's from Sierra Leone and he speaks French, English, and Swahili. All fluently. He doesn't talk a lot, but he likes Travis. They do the majority of contact tracing for us, so they are together fairly often. Maybe he'd know more."

Damon pulled her to a stop at the edge of the burned village. The tents and structures of the village burned fast so that in the short walk, there was nothing left but burning piles. The smoke was a dark cloud and the acrid smell of what was left burned her nose.

Anuma was nowhere to be seen.

"I just don't understand," she said, staring at the devastation.

"And maybe you never will. For now, let's see if we can salvage anything from your tent and get back to base. Lead the way."

Dani admired the way Damon could focus on only what was important at the moment, whereas she had been so overwhelmed with questions and sadness that she'd felt rooted to the spot, unable to go forward or back.

"It's on the other side, near the temporary hospital tent."

Damon turned her toward him, holding out a bandana. "Put this over your nose and mouth; it'll help with the smoke."

"Okay," she mumbled.

"We'll figure it out, Dani. I promise."

She looked into his light topaz eyes and immediately felt safe. He would take care of it, because she couldn't. It wasn't something she understood. Dani worked to save people, to make their lives better. Not destroy them. Or destroy their way of lives. How could Anuma do something like this?

She took a deep breath through the bandana, finding that the smoke wasn't as bad with that filter on. Then she nodded and led the way through the burning piles, picking her way around fallen structures and burning clothing.

The tent she'd shared with Hailey and Claire was a bit further away from the others and was where she'd seen Anuma standing before they'd landed. He'd dropped the torch, probably hoping it would light up as well, but only one side of the structure had burned completely. The rest was smoldering.

Dani ducked inside before Damon could stop her and searched for her bag of samples that she'd kept under her cot. It wasn't there.

"What the hell were you thinking?" Damon said, right before the iron bar that was his arm snaked around her waist. She was pulled up and back against him as he got them out of the tent.

There was a popping noise and then the whole thing fell over sideways. Small flames grew into larger ones as fire began to consume the spot she'd just been standing in.

"I'm sorry; I didn't realize—"

"That the whole damn thing was about to come down on your head?"

Dani turned in his arms, trying to take a step back, but he wasn't going for it. "Thank you for pulling me out."

Damon pulled on her braid, forcing her face up to his, and her breath caught because she thought he might kiss her. It was a silly whim, but she wished he would. Her heart was beating faster from the near miss with the collapse. It couldn't be because her body was flush against his, feeling all that hard, hot flesh against her softer body.

"Do not do that again."

His tone was hard and he emphasized every word. And only once did his eyes stray from hers. But when they did, they focused on her lips and made them tingle.

"Want us to chase the fire bug, Shadow?"

The lance corporal's voice cut into the moment, but Dani was glad it broke the spell. Damon let go of her and she moved away to steady herself. She tuned out the conversation, turning her mind instead to her missing bag and the mystery of why a good man would set fire to an entire village.

CHAPTER 7

"How did it go at the village?" Claire asked, as Dani sat down with a plate of food.

They were in the mess tent where soldiers and medical staff filed in and out, eating and socializing. The food was unimaginative, but it was hot and tasted decent. It was lunch time and she was hungry, having slept through breakfast. It had been a long and depressing flight back from Ghana.

"How does everyone know where we went?" Claire was the second person to ask that since she'd picked up her food.

Claire rolled her eyes. "How do you think?"

"Hailey?" It was a guess, but Hailey tended to know more than she should in any given situation.

"Yep." Claire poked at the brown mass on her plate. "She used those baby blues to weasel the info out of a horny radio operator." She stabbed at the food again. "What *is* this?"

"That is military meatloaf," Damon said, sitting down across from the two women.

"It's almost un-edible in the hands of a less talented cook," Gunner continued, sitting down beside Damon.

"Is it really meatloaf?" Claire asked.

"No one actually knows," Gunner said, winking at her. "But you can live on it."

"Where's the rest of the team?" Damon asked.

Dani saw the slow scan of the crowd that he did, looking for the rest of her crew. She'd looked herself and didn't see Travis, Hailey, or Martin. And who knew where Anuma had taken off to? He'd disappeared so thoroughly that the soldiers had lost his trail at the edge of the jungle.

"I haven't seen anyone but Claire since we landed," she said.

Claire's nose scrunched as she sniffed the white lump that looked like mashed potatoes. She took an experimental bite before saying, "Travis is sulking in his tent. I saw him leaving as I was coming in for food."

"What's he upset about?" Dani asked. She was steadily eating for the fuel, and it wasn't as bad as it looked.

"He doesn't like not knowing where you went. And, if you ask me, he's jealous," Claire said.

"Someone has a bit of unrequited love, huh?" Gunner grinned at Dani.

His plate was already clear, as was Damon's. They didn't waste any time on the meal either. Damon leaned forward on his elbows, fixed on the conversation. His hair swept forward over his forehead and Dani had the ridiculous urge to reach over and push it back. His hair was longer than normal, but he'd always been the rebellious one of his family. At least, that's what Gabriel always said. She thought that maybe he was a bit envious of his wilder brother.

"Who even says that—" Claire laughed, "—unrequited?"

Damon grinned and said, "Well—"

Gunner shoved him, "Don't do it."

"He reads Victorian romance novels when he's bored."

Dani stared at the man, who now had a faint redness around his ears. Gunner Halverson, she knew, was a man

51

of many talents. He was wealthy from inheritance as well as from his own inventions, had a doctorate from M.I.T., and regularly consulted on top secret government problems. The nature of those, well, no one really knew about except for a few key people very high up in the pecking order.

And, on top of it all, he was drop dead gorgeous.

"Wait, you read romance novels?" Claire asked. Then covered her mouth as she laughed. "You *so* do not look the type."

Damon continued ruthlessly, "And paranormal romance."

Dani bit her lip to keep the laughter inside. It felt good to smile about something, and Gunner's rapidly darkening complexion was becoming hilarious. She cleared her throat before saying, "I think it's nice that you read widely."

Gunner elbowed Damon. "He reads the same books."

Damon grinned, not the least bit embarrassed. "I only read books by Elizabeth Richardson, and only because Zach makes me."

Claire gasped. "I love her books." She turned and looked at Dani. "She's the one I told you about that writes that psychic detective series. I have all seven of those books and am rabidly waiting on book eight."

"Yeah, well, our buddy Zach is married to her, and he makes us buy every single one." Gunner's face was still pink around the cheeks.

Damon shrugged, "They're great books."

"True, but knowing the main character is based on Zach makes reading the sex scenes just awkward," Gunner said.

Dani laughed out loud this time, imagining these two tough guys reading some steamy romance love scene while trying not to imagine their friend. She envied them that closeness, that willingness to buy a book in support of their friend's wife, and even read it. She only had that with Claire, and only because they'd been on so many assignments together.

Through the mesh of the tent entrance, Dani saw Travis walk by. She wanted to catch him and find out what was going on with him. Maybe get a feel for where his head was at. She stood up and grabbed her tray.

"I'm sorry to leave abruptly, but there's someone I need to speak to."

Damon stood. "I'll come with you."

Dani shook her head and motioned for him to sit back down. "This is something I need to do alone." She could tell he didn't like that answer, but he reluctantly sat back down.

"Don't worry, I'll keep these two occupied for you, Dani." Claire winked at her and nodded toward the door.

She'd obviously seen Travis as well and knew Dani wanted to talk to him. Walking toward the front, she dumped her tray off and headed outside. She caught sight of Travis as he rounded the corner, a towel thrown over his shoulder and his shower bag in one hand. She wanted to catch him before he got to the showers.

"Hey, Travis, wait up."

He stopped at the sound of her voice. Hers was a bit low for a woman, rich and smoky, and it had followed him into more than one of his more erotic dreams about her. He'd stopped in the shadows and waited for her to catch up to him.

"I've been looking for you," she said.

If only. "Well, you found me. What's up?"

She reached out and touched his arm. The same way Hailey had hours before, only this time, his body lit up in a way that it only did when Dani touched him. Oh, he knew

Hailey had a thing for him, but that would pass. She got infatuated with any guy she was in contact with for more than a couple of hours. She was a kid. Dani was a woman.

A woman he'd been patient with, hoping she'd finally see him as a man. Not a co-worker.

"Are you okay?" she asked. "You haven't seemed like yourself lately, and with everything that's happened, I wanted to touch base with you and make sure you were alright."

She removed her hand as casually as she'd touched him, and he missed the warmth she left behind. Dani rarely touched anyone, so he took that as a good sign.

"Actually, I'm worried about you."

She looked surprised. "I'm fine."

"Are you? Taking off with that Damon guy isn't safe, Dani."

Waving her hand in a dismissive gesture, she said, "He's a safe pilot. And we had five of the military guys with us as an escort. Perfectly safe."

Travis ran a hand through his hair. It was frustrating trying to talk to Dani about anything except work. That was the only thing she wasn't closed up about. "I'm not talking about flying back to the damn village, Dani. Even though that wasn't a good idea; I'm talking about Damon himself. He's not safe."

Her big green eyes glowed in the semi darkness, drawing him toward her. He had to make her understand, and he wanted to be close to her. He always wanted to be close to her. But she took a step back, putting space between them again.

"I don't know what you're talking about, Travis. And I don't think you do either."

"He's a killer, damn it. Did you know that? He's a mercenary with orders to protect that Dr. Halverson with whatever means necessary. And he was a sniper. I heard some of the soldiers talking, practically worshiping him because he shoots people from far away. It's disgusting. He's got blood on his hands."

Travis couldn't tell what she was thinking. Her face was completely blank. Maybe she was in shock at hearing that her brother-in-law was completely different from the noble man that was her late husband. A man that was like Travis. Both doctors. Both willing to sacrifice their lives to save others. And both in love with Danielle Bordeaux.

He dropped his bag and reached out to grip her shoulders. To force her to understand that Damon was beneath her, beneath them both.

"Let me go, Travis."

"You save lives and he takes them. How can you look at him the way you do when he kills for a living? You're so much better than he is."

"You're hurting me, Travis. Let. Me. Go."

"Let her go, now, or I'll show you exactly how much of a killer I am," Damon said, his voice washing over Travis like a cold wave. "And it'll be up close and personal."

Dani backed away, the look on her face wasn't directed at Damon the way it should have been. Instead, she was looking at him with dread. While rubbing her arms. He hadn't meant to hurt her. *Oh, God, never that.*

"I'm sorry, Dani. I didn't mean to scare you."

She said nothing.

Then, Travis looked at the man he'd just called a killer. And any thoughts of being able to handle himself were immediately discarded. Cold dread washed over him. He was no match for the very angry man standing almost in front of Dani now, protecting her from Travis himself. That wasn't how it was supposed to be. She was supposed to realize that Damon was the threat, not look at him like he was.

"You ever touch her again, Travis, and I'll rip your arms off and beat you to death with them. Am I perfectly clear?"

He hated himself for nodding, for giving in and looking weak in front of Dani. But he didn't have a choice. He believed the man in front of him. There was no doubt in Travis's mind that if he ever touched Dani again, he was a dead man.

~

CLAIRE DREW BACK into the shadows of the nearest tent. She hadn't meant to follow anyone; she had merely headed back to her own sleeping space, the one she shared with Hailey, when she'd come up on the end of that little confrontation.

Travis picked up his shower bag and scuttled away, tail tucked firmly between his legs, as far as she could tell. And Damon grabbed Dani's hand and led her in the opposite direction. Her friend looked a little shell shocked by the whole thing.

"Spying?"

Claire turned her head, barely able to see the sarcastic little smile on Dr. Graham's face. "More like, not wanting to interrupt that rather tense little scene. Besides, what're you doing skulking around in the shadows?"

The smile dropped off his face. "I do not skulk, Ms. Belgarde. I was also merely going this way."

"Your tent isn't this way," she said. She crossed her arms over her chest and stared at him. He could be such a formal ass.

"No, but the infirmary is, and we might have a new Ebola case. I was asked to come and consult, since Dr. Bordeaux couldn't be located. Clearly, she is sorting out some personal issues."

Claire snorted at him, not caring that he raised his

eyebrows at the unladylike noise. "What new Ebola case? I was there most of the day and it was all routine vaccinations."

"The man who came in with the head wound. He's the one."

"But, they were all tested," she said. None of the villagers had shown any signs of being positive for the virus. No one even had so much as a fever. "We'd better tell Dani."

"Not yet," Martin said. "Let's make sure it's actually something to be worried about and not Dr. Montgomery trying to cause a panic."

"Then, let's go. I want to see this for myself."

This was seriously going to derail all their plans for going stateside if it really was Ebola in the camp. They'd all need to follow quarantine procedures, which would keep them in Liberia another twenty-one days.

CHAPTER 8

$\mathcal{D}$amon was vibrating with the need to punch something. Travis was his focus, but he knew Dani wouldn't want him to seriously hurt a teammate and friend. And right now, he was in a killing mood. Seeing his hands on Dani—hurting her.

He had her smaller hand in his as Damon led them toward her tent. She was the only thing keeping him from finding that bastard again and showing him what hurt was. And she was too quiet, not stopping him from dragging her through camp. That worried him.

She should be giving him all kinds of hell.

When he had her safely inside, he closed the door and dropped the cloth blinds to ensure privacy. "Dani?"

Her face was expressionless, but her cheeks were pink and she was blinking rapidly, trying to hold back tears. Damon made the effort to calm down, taking a deep breath, before lifting his hand to her chin and tilting her face up to his.

"Are you alright?"

She nodded, the move jerky, and tried to move away.

"Fine," she whispered.

"You're not fine. Did he hurt you?"

She rubbed her arms and shook her head. "Just a little."

One tear broke free and slid down her cheek and that was more than Damon could take. He pulled her into his arms and held her close. "It's okay to cry, sugar. A lot has happened in the last two days."

Her sob nearly broke his heart. He scooped her up into his arms and sat them both onto her cot. With her face buried in his neck and her arms up around his neck, he couldn't think of anywhere else he'd rather be. And she felt damn good in his arms.

Better than he'd ever imagined. Over the years, he'd imagined more than he'd ever admit to anyone. He gently unbraided her hair and ran his fingers through it in long strokes. He knew she found it soothing when she sighed.

"I'm sorry," she sniffed.

"Shush. You have yourself a good cry."

Dani hadn't lifted her head from his shoulder, so he couldn't see her face, but he could feel her start to shake. With laughter. He pulled back so he could see her expression. It was tear-stained, and her cheeks were almost as red as her hair. But those big green eyes are what held him.

"I think I needed that." She ducked her head and continued to smile. "But now I'm feeling really stupid for being curled up in your lap like a little girl."

He grinned. Very glad she was getting her spunk back. "Got my shirt all wet too."

"That's what you get for being all macho and sweet." She was wiping away the moisture around her eyes, which was beginning to dry up, with the sleeve of her shirt.

Damon couldn't help but turn serious. He'd heard what Travis said and he wasn't wrong. Dani was a healer, and he'd taken more lives than he could even talk about. But she wasn't looking at him like he was some kind of pariah.

"I have taken lives, Dani. Travis isn't wrong about me. It was my job. Still is."

Her eyes widened and then she reached up to smooth the hair from his forehead. It was a tender gesture. One he hadn't expected, but it felt nice.

"You protected the men on your team, Damon. That's what you do." She frowned as she looked at the door. "What Travis said was—"

She shifted in his lap and froze. There was no mistaking what was rapidly happening in his pants. He'd been able to control himself while she'd been upset and crying it out. But now, the smell of her hair and the feel of her curvy, warm body was bringing out his baser instincts. She wasn't even wearing any expensive perfume, just plain soap and her own unique fragrance. It was a heady combination.

"Maybe I should move," she said. Her eyebrow was arched and her frown had turned a tad mischievous.

Damon stifled a groan. "If you move any more, this situation is going to change your perception of me from caring knight-in-shining-armor to something a lot less complimentary, given recent events."

DANI DIDN'T WANT to move, and yet she did. The safe feeling she had in his arms was quickly turning into something else. Something much more complicated.

Damon's light topaz eyes had turned dark and serious. And the rigid length of him was snug against her bottom, making her heart thud in her chest. A heart that until this moment, she thought might be encased in ice.

"Finish what you were going to say about Travis," he said. And if his voice was husky now, she tried to ignore it.

"He's just wrong. You aren't a killer." She reached up and cupped his cheek, knowing he needed to hear this. Because it was obvious that he believed the same thing Travis did. She had to make him understand that what he'd done was necessary and even noble.

"You made hard choices and served your country with honor. Screw what Travis said and anyone else who thinks that way."

She stared into his eyes, willing him to believe her. But then his eyes moved down to her lips and she realized that both of her hands were around his neck and her face was mere inches from his. If she moved any closer, she'd be plastered up against him.

"I warned you," he rasped.

Then his lips touched hers. And it surprised her so much that she gasped and he slipped his tongue inside and took over. He was a conquering warrior and she was a prize fought for and won.

Dani melted.

His arms were around her in a second and she was taken. Her breasts pressed against his muscled chest, tingling and tightening in an almost painfully sweet sensation. Dani's fingers tunneled into his long hair as his found her own.

The kiss was a warm and wet explosion of taste. It was as if she'd been seeing in black and white her whole life and suddenly could see in color. Her body lit up, feelings she thought long dead rising eagerly to the surface.

The sounds she made in the back of her throat would probably embarrass her later, but at this moment, they were totally involuntary.

"Goddamn, you taste good," he said.

"Hmm." She wasn't sure she was actually capable of words

because he started kissing her again and it was so good she never wanted to stop.

She'd been on some dates over the years, even shared some kisses, but none of those had inspired much more than a pleasant warmth. Nothing like the volcanic need raging through her veins. And just being in his arms, so strong and so gentle, made her want to cry again. And that was the problem. She needed him in a way that she shouldn't. Dani couldn't do this. She just couldn't.

She pulled away. "I'm sorry. That shouldn't have happened."

Damon kissed her again, a quick swipe of his lips. "Why the hell not?"

"Because it isn't right. It reminds me too much—"

"Of Gabriel," he finished.

She scooted off his lap to pace the floor, mainly because the feel of him was a temptation she was dangerously close to throwing herself at. And how could he not remind her of her dead husband? They were twins, for God's sake.

"Listen, Damon—" she started, but a loud pounding on the door stopped her.

"Hope you're decent. I'm coming in," Gunner Halverson said before opening the door.

He stopped just inside, briefcase in one hand and a smirk on his face. A quick look at their disheveled appearance and it was clear there had been something going on. Dani could feel the tips of her ears get hot.

"What's up, Gun?" Damon asked. He didn't bother to straighten up, just sat there and looked at both of them.

"Sorry to interrupt, folks, but we have a situation." His grin said he wasn't sorry at all, but his eyes were serious as he set the briefcase down and began entering the combination for the locks.

Damon stood at that point, but Dani wasn't sure what was going on. "What's the situation?" she asked.

"Seems we have an Ebola case in the infirmary."

"What?" Dani shook her head. "But everyone was tested when they came into the camp. There was nothing but routine cases."

Gunner nodded as he popped the locks and opened the case. "That's why we need to get some samples now. I have a feeling your mutated strand is here now."

Inside the case was soft padding that encased two vials of a milky white liquid and a number of syringes. Gunner began loading up three of those syringes in rapid succession, showing no hesitation as he turned toward her with one of the needles.

"What is that?" she asked. It wasn't something she was familiar with, especially since there was no label on the vial. She'd moved closer to look.

"This is the reason I'm here, to study the virus and come up with an antidote, if possible. Those vials are a prototype that I refined for the CDC that they've been being testing on monkeys. I'd planned on using mine once we'd rounded up some sample subjects to see if there was some measurable success."

"So, why are you looking at us like we're now your guinea pigs?" Damon asked. He crossed his arms over his chest and glared at the needle.

"Jesus, Damon, you've been shot twice and fly that chopper of yours like you have a death wish. You're really going to give me a hard time about a little needle stick?"

"Why the fuck are you planning on giving us shots?"

The grimace and wary tone pulled a reluctant smile out of Dani. She hadn't known Damon had a fear of needles. But he did have a valid question.

Gunner answered before she could put her question with

Damon's. "This is something I've been working on that is preventative as well as reactive. Obviously, top secret and not something even the higher ups know about. I brought enough for myself and Damon, just in case. But I can stretch it to cover the three of us."

Dani knew her jaw was about to drop. The top minds in the pharmaceutical companies, as well as government, were working on something similar, but she'd heard of no advances yet. "How did you get approval to work on this?"

He shrugged, "I didn't. But I was one of the original doctors that began working on it when it became an epidemic, and I was the one that made all the progress. Now, roll up your sleeves."

"You're not injecting me with whatever that is, Gun." Damon backed away a step.

"If I have to hold you down and have Dani here do it, then I will. At least three of us will have a chance against this virus. And we might be the difference between life and death for this camp."

His eyes were narrowed, and there was a tick in his jaw, but Damon didn't comment. Dani turned the attention back to herself, "I don't know what that is and I'm with Damon. You're not injecting me with it."

Gunner had short sleeves, so instead of answering the questions, he merely injected himself with the first syringe. Once he was done, he put a bandage on and then picked up a second syringe. "Look, I'm one of the brightest minds out there and I don't give a shit about government regulation. They only want a preventable solution for American troops and doctors. I don't think the big brass care one way or the other if everyone here dies or not. But I do. And I believe everyone deserves a cure."

"I don't think that's true; they care. They've been working on a cure for years now," Dani protested. She believed in what she was doing. She believed in the CDC, even though they hadn't made any real strides yet in finding that cure for humans.

"True or not, I want to be able to help, and this is part of what I'm working on. This anti-virus won't do any damage, and it just might stop us from getting infected. And if this is your mutated virus, we need all the help we can get."

"You can trust him, Dani." Damon was still glaring at the needle in Gunner's hand, but his voice was calm, and something about his faith made her believe.

"You really think this will work?" she asked.

Gunner nodded. "It can't hurt, and we've got to figure out what is going on before the infection begins to spread."

"Do you have any more? What about the rest of my team?"

Dani rolled up her sleeve and Gunner stabbed the needle in before she changed her mind. The pinch lasted only a moment before he was done and applying the bandage.

"I don't have enough to inoculate anyone else. I'm sorry, Dani, but everyone else will have to use normal precautions when handling the sick. I'm also going to want to check our blood and take samples as well, which means more needles, tough guy. My lab is up and running, so I will be able to synthesize this serum, but it will take some time."

Damon had taken a couple of silent steps toward the door. Dani hadn't even noticed. She'd been too intent on making the decision to accept the shot. She reached out and grabbed his hand. "You need to do this too. Especially since you talked me into trusting your friend."

"I don't have to like this," Damon said. He squeezed her hand and let her roll up his sleeve. All the muscles bulged in his arm as he stood stock still and waited.

"Stop being a baby and relax or this is going to hurt more than it needs to," Gunner said.

"Just fucking get it over with, asshat."

Dani smothered another smile and held onto his hand. He was being a baby, but it was kind of cute as well. That such a tough guy was scared of needles was endearing and made him more human in her eyes. Not that kissing the socks right off of her hadn't done the same thing, but she'd always viewed him in the way someone views a wild animal. With respect and from a distance.

He sucked in a breath as Gunner gave him the shot, but he stood still. His thumb rubbed across her knuckles back and forth, betraying his agitation, but overall, he did well. Taking the bandage from Gunner, Dani applied it to Damon's arm and then leaned in and gave his arm a quick kiss.

He smiled down at her, "Thanks for kissing it better, Red. It barely hurts anymore."

"I'm running back to my tent to drop this off. Dani, meet me in the infirmary. Damon, I need you to find out where the hell Dani's team has been today and yesterday." Gunner snapped the case closed and spun the numbers in the lock.

"I'm on it," Damon said, as Gunner disappeared. Then he turned back to Dani. "You and I aren't done with our discussion."

Dani knew he was talking about the kiss and what she'd said before Gunner came barging in. But it all came down to her being lonely. She was a woman in her prime and she missed having that special someone in her life. She missed sex. But she didn't want Damon to be a stand in for his dead twin. That would be wrong. And she couldn't use him that way.

"I just can't Damon, that's all."

"I haven't stopped thinking about that kiss, Dani. The one we shared before you got married. The one that damned near melted my mama's wallpaper right off the walls. I wasn't a stand in, and you know it."

Then he left and she was alone. As much as she tried to deny it to herself over the years, what he said was true. She had known. Oh, it had started out a mistake that was helped by a dark room and a little too much champagne. But she'd known. And had dared to taste the wilder Dupree.

Now she was afraid. Afraid she'd become addicted. And she knew she'd never survive loss like that again.

CHAPTER 9

*T*he atmosphere inside the infirmary was one of
focused attention and consternation. Dani heard
one of the nurses asking how Ebola could have been missed
and whose ass was going to get chewed out for that mistake.

"Dr. Bordeaux, I'm glad you're here," Dr. Montgomery
Nelson said. "I need a consult on these symptoms."

"Please, call me Dani," she said. She was already suited up,
including mask and gloves, since they had made a special
area outside the tent with those supplies once they realized
that one of the patients had Ebola. No one would enter this
building without precautions.

"This patient came in one week ago with a severe head
injury. He had a slight infection due to the trauma, but
nothing else. Now, he suddenly, inexplicably, has the virus."

"And there is something unusual about the symptoms?"

Monty shot her a quick look. "What, are you psychic now,
too?"

"No, but I have a theory and that could be a huge problem
for us. Let me examine the patient and take some samples."

She could tell Monty wanted some answers, but was

professional enough to wait and let her do the exam. "Dr. Halverson is already taking samples now."

They weaved around tables and cots to an area that was cordoned off with some industrial strength plastic that was opaque enough to obscure whatever it shielded. The strong odor of disinfectant permeated the air. This was a sterile place that would be cleaned even more regularly due to the threat of spreading the deadly disease.

"Perfect," she said.

The patient was a man in his middle thirties. Monty rattled off the stats he had, including the fact that he'd not regained consciousness since he'd been brought in. A bright white gauze bandage covered his head, contrasting brightly with his deep black skin. Monitors were on his fingers and chest, and an IV had been inserted in the top of his left hand.

Gunner was drawing several vials of blood, similarly garbed in the white biohazard suit, large goggles and mask in place. "His fever is already at one hundred and four. And if you move the sheet, he has recent skin lesions on his stomach and thighs."

"It's moving fast," she murmured. Moving the sheet, she saw the lesions. Replacing the cover, she moved to his head and opened one eye.

Blood seeped from the corner and the entire eye was bloodshot, pupils barely contracting in her pen light. It could only be day two, and yesterday would have been the only day her people had access to this tent. Damn. She'd been holding out a foolish hope that the village would have been the end of it.

Clearly, it was only the beginning.

"I must have missed something," Monty said. "I checked all these people out myself when we got here."

He was shaking his head and staring at the blood still

seeping from the eye of the poor man dying in front of them. The virus was already advanced.

"I don't think you did, Doc," Gunner said. He packed up the vials of blood he'd taken, as well as a tissue sample from one of the skin lesions. "This is something else. Something worse."

"He should have shown symptoms before now. He's been here for a week now, and while I've been worried about the coma he's in, he wasn't showing any signs of infection."

Dani moved around the man in the bed and touched Monty's arm, drawing his fixed attention from the patient. "I think you did everything you could, but this is a new infection."

"How the hell could this be new? He's in the advanced stages." He still looked bewildered. Finally, he said, "I hope he doesn't wake up to feel the pain."

Glancing at Gunner, she saw him nod and decided to take Montgomery into her confidence. There was no way he could be involved, and he needed to be aware of the risks and ready for more. "It's new because *we* are new in camp."

He frowned at her, but stayed quiet, willing to listen.

"I'm worried that someone has mutated the virus. Making it stronger and faster."

Monty just blinked. Dani didn't blame him; it had taken her awhile to get used to the idea that a doctor was deliberately doing this. "That can't be right," he said.

"We'll know for sure once I can look at these samples." Gunner was packed and headed toward the front. "My lab is set up next to the command tent and I've asked for it to be guarded. No one goes in except for me."

Montgomery nodded. "I understand."

Dani watched him as his eyes widened and his head swung back to her. "Someone on your team?" She had a feeling he'd be quick on the uptake. "But who? I've met everyone and I thought you all an extraordinary group. Your people were here helping me not that long ago. Claire and Dr. Graham."

"I thought so too. All of us have been in here helping out at different times, so I can't even narrow it down that way, with the exception of our guide, Anuma, who disappeared after we arrived." And what he'd been doing was still a mystery to her and Damon. But it was possible that he'd slipped inside the infirmary to infect the patient before he left.

"That's a serious charge, Dani. Once that gets out, your careers might be over."

She'd thought about that already, which is why she hadn't gone to the commander of this unit. Not that life didn't come before any of their reputations, but she didn't want to start a panic before she had proof, and she wasn't likely to be believed anyway.

Hopefully, Gunner had the proof in his vials.

Otherwise, Dr. Montgomery Nelson's reputation would be shredded as well, because he'd misdiagnosed or outright missed a case of Ebola that could potentially affect everyone in the camp. All of his nurses and staff had some kind of contact with patient zero in the last week, though they could narrow the field a bit for those that cared for the man in the last two days.

"I have to have the proof. Once I have that, then I can take the steps to handle the problem. Until then, we have to work on containment. I don't want to lose anyone else and this is a large camp."

"The casualties to life would be severe if it's working this fast," Monty said. He headed toward the door. "I need to call a meeting with my people and work out a strategy."

"And, Monty?"

He stopped and turned, "Yes?"

Dani still had a hand on the patient. She wanted to look him over more thoroughly. "Let's keep this between ourselves for now."

"Of course," he said. And then he headed toward the decontamination area.

Placing a hand gently on the un-bandaged part of the sick man's head, Dani whispered, "Who did this to you?" And wished he could give her the answer she needed.

THERE WERE VERY few things Damon actually missed about being an active Marine, but the camaraderie was one. Civilian life paid better, the food was better, and the freedom to come and go as he damn well pleased was worth it. And when he found himself working around other branches of the military, he was the odd man out. But not with the Corps.

Once you were a Marine, you were always a Marine.

And when you were a sniper with a larger than average amount of kills, respect was a given. They knew of him. Which was why he could move in and around the guys, asking questions, and no one gave it a second thought. He was one of them, always would be, and he genuinely liked most of the guys he'd run into so far.

The exception was Sergeant Larry Clemons.

"Yeah, I saw her. Nice ass, but her tits are on the small side."

Damon stifled the urge to deck the Sergeant, just on general principle. He was one of those rich boys that came in and thought they knew how to handle the rest of the grunts. The man was also a misogynistic asshole, but he'd been the only one to actually remember seeing Hailey last night.

"So, she was over in the radio tent the last you saw her?" Damon asked.

"Yeah, she was putting those little titties in Private First Class Jenson's face. Fine with me, he's a good kid and could use a quick lay. Me, I'd like a piece of that curvy little redheaded doctor."

Damon smiled, even though he could feel his fist clench with the need to bury it in Clemons' face. "She's off limits."

That got the sergeant's attention. "Yeah? Damn."

"Yeah," he said.

It was almost a growl when it came out. *She's mine.* It was guttural and basic, and he'd never let himself think that way before, but it was there, pulsing under the surface. He wanted her. And maybe it was a twin thing after all, because Gabriel had said he'd wanted her the moment he saw her.

She'd been like a punch in the gut when Damon had seen her the first time.

He'd never been possessive before, but just the thought of this prick thinking anything about Dani made Damon want to break his face. Slowly. Painfully.

The Sergeant raised his hands in a conciliatory gesture. "Hey, no problem. I got a thing going with one of those nurses anyway. She's more to my taste," he said. Then made a motion showing that the woman in question obviously had a larger bust size.

Damon rolled his shoulders to ease the tension, now that he was sure the Sergeant wasn't going to be a problem. "What about the others? Have you seen any of them?"

"Just Doctor Dickhead and that stuck up chick with the dark red hair. Cara or Clarice or something." He shook himself in a mock shiver, making the noise. "That one could freeze off your pecker just looking at her."

"Claire?"

"Maybe, didn't really pay attention to her name."

The urge to just shoot the idiot in front of him was getting harder to ignore, but Damon was making the effort.

His mama would've flayed him alive if she'd ever caught him talking about women that way this sergeant was. Not to mention, he genuinely liked women, and this turd gave all guys a bad name.

But all he said was, "What were they doing?"

"Having an argument about something. I was too far away to hear it, but the Ice Queen looked pissed and then they went separate ways."

"Where were they when this happened?"

The sergeant shrugged. "Outside the medical tent. I was headed that way to meet that nurse I was talking about. They'd just come out."

Damon nodded. "Thanks for the info, Sergeant. I won't keep you from your date."

How the nurse in question put up with that ass, Damon didn't know, but clearly she saw something that he was missing. A lot of the "guy" talk about women was macho bullshit, said to impress other guys in most cases. But that sergeant was the genuine article. Probably didn't get held enough as a child.

Putting it from his mind, Damon went in search of Hailey. No one remembered seeing her since last night and that was unusual. The tent she shared with Claire was empty. Neither woman had much, but Hailey had her stuff strewn around everywhere. He searched through it all.

And found nothing suspicious.

Next, he went to the first large tent that housed the grunts. Sticking his head inside, he found one of the guys reading a book. "Hey, buddy, have you seen Jenson?"

The kid looked up. Couldn't have been more than twenty and reading a spy thriller. "The radio guy?"

"That'd be him."

"He's in B Company. They're in the next tent over."

"Hey, thanks."

The kid said, "No problem." Then he buried his nose back in his book.

Damon found Private First Class Jenson in the last cot, in the back of the tent assigned to B Company. He was asleep, but the sweat dotting his forehead and the grimace on his face wasn't good. Putting a hand Jenson's head, Damon felt the heat coming off of him.

"Shit." He shook the kid. "Jenson, wake up."

His eyes popped open and Damon could see the glazed look. "I don't feel good," he moaned. Then he rolled to his side and started puking.

"Oh, hell," Damon said and jumped back. This was bad. There were two other soldiers in the tent with them and they'd jumped up at the noise and were beginning to come back toward Damon. He held out a hand and motioned for them to stop.

"Both of you out of the tent. Now. And someone go get either Dr. Nelson or Dr. Bordeaux. Whoever stays, don't let anyone else inside this tent."

One of them said he would stand guard and the other took off for the infirmary. The smell of vomit permeated the air and it was a good thing Damon had an iron stomach, otherwise he'd have been retching right alongside Jenson. Poor kid puked more than a body could possibly hold, but then he rolled onto his back, one arm covering his eyes.

"How long have you been sick?" Damon asked.

But no answer was coming, because Jenson started jerking and wheezing. His eyes rolled back and he was in a full seizure. One hand flailed up and knocked over everything on the nightstand, so Damon pulled it away so the kid wouldn't hit his head. He knew not to attempt to restrain him, not wishing to hurt the kid or get hurt himself.

It felt longer than it was, but soon Dani was there with Dr. Nelson, both suited up with full biohazard gear.

"Damon." She breathed his name softly through her mask, but he could hear the worry. Chances were the private was infected and here Damon was in unprotected contact with him.

"Just help him, Dani. Don't worry about me." *Yet.* But he didn't say it out loud. Didn't even want to think it. He just prayed Gunner's concoction protected him.

"Did he say anything?" she asked. Both her and Dr. Nelson had begun taking his temp and checking his vitals.

"When I got here, he was asleep, but burning up. I shook him awake and he said that he didn't feel good, then started throwing up, and then went into a seizure. The seizure lasted about a minute. He was never really conscious."

"We have to move him to the infirmary," Dr. Nelson said.

"That will take time, Monty. We have to have more people suited up."

Damon knew it was urgent to isolate the kid before infection spread, and since he was already potentially at risk, he said, "I'll carry him. You just keep everyone back."

"Damn it, Damon," she said.

He laid a hand on her arm and looked at worried green eyes encased in those huge plastic goggles. "I'm already exposed, sugar. Might as well make use of me."

When she reluctantly nodded, he pulled Jenson up by the arms, put his shoulder into his stomach, and hoisted the kid over his shoulder in a fireman carry. He just hoped the kid didn't puke all over him. "Lead the way."

They passed the two soldiers that had been in the tent with Jenson. Damon waved them over. "You two need to come with us and get checked out."

"What's going on, sir?" The younger one said.

"We have Ebola in the camp," Damon said. "The three of us need to get checked out along with Jenson here."

The other soldier said, "Shit. How the hell did that happen? We haven't been anywhere near the villagers."

"Not sure, but let's just make sure we don't have it, and then figure out the rest."

They muttered between themselves, but followed along. At a distance. The instant fear in their voices pissed Damon off. These kids hadn't signed up for a monster with a pet virus. They looked barely out of high school. When he found who was doing this, he wasn't sure he could wait for justice to prevail. And it wouldn't be the first time he'd taken matters into his own hands.

Once inside the medical tent, he headed for the heavy plastic. Dr. Monty Nelson had run ahead and was busy moving a bed over and away from the other beds. The rest of the hospital staff had been busy setting up a new infirmary on the other side of the camp for normal maladies and injuries. This tent was now the containment area.

He settled Jenson and turned to leave. Dani's hand on his arm stopped him.

"I need a sample of your blood," she said.

He flinched, but nodded. "Alright, but be quick. I have a call to make and I need to find Hailey, since she was the last one seen with Jenson."

"You need to stay here with the other two soldiers, Damon. You've been exposed."

He could feel himself grimace at her words. He knew that. "This whole damn place has been exposed at this point, Dani. Jenson was a radio operator in the command tent and had dinner tonight with A and B Company in the chow hall. Who do you think he hasn't been in contact with?"

She sighed. "You're right, but that doesn't mean I don't want to keep an eye on you."

"You can keep your eyes all over me, anytime you want."

That dragged a reluctant smile out of her, just like he

hoped. He was serious, but he gave her a wink and a smile as he sat down next to her work area. "But for now, draw some blood and let me go find Hailey."

"You think she did this?"

"I think she's on my suspect list, especially since no one has seen her for hours."

"She might be sick, Damon."

He nodded. He'd thought about that too, in which case, she needed to be found ASAP. "I'll find her, Dani."

"Thank you."

After she'd taken a vial of blood and marked his name on it, he stood and put his hands on her shoulders, pulling her in for a quick hug. "You be careful, Red."

"This is what I do, Damon. It's what I'm good at."

"I know you are. And I'm headed out to do what I'm good at."

"You planning on killing someone?" Her whisper was low and playful, but he could see the worry in her eyes.

"That's not the only thing I'm good at. I also play a mean game of poker."

"And fly helicopters."

"See, I'm good at all kinds of things."

With a last squeeze of her shoulders through the bunny suit, he slipped out of the tent. He planned to avoid anyone he came into contact with, but he wanted his scope and the SAT phone.

He had a call to make.

CHAPTER 10

The call picked up after the second ring. "Yeah?"

"Tell me you have something for me, Mike," Damon said. He was up on the same hill in some scrubby brush that provided some decent cover. He had the SAT phone to one ear and a scope to one eye. Night vision goggles would have been better, but he was damned good without them, so he'd just grabbed the scope for this outing.

"I have some. I'll have more when Zach and Jesse check in."

"What are they doing?"

Mike chuckled. "What they do best. Breaking and entering."

Damon could appreciate the irony. As the owners of J.Z. Alarms and Consultation, Jesse and Zach were paid to break into high security homes and businesses to assess the weaknesses of the already installed alarms. They'd yet to run into an alarm that Zach couldn't disable within three minutes. And Jesse was a genius at designing unique, and impenetrable, alarms for those same businesses. He was also good with some computer hacking.

"And where are they breaking and entering?"

"Atlanta."

Damon didn't bother worrying about his friends. They were the best at what they did. And he had a good idea what they might be doing in the city that played host to the CDC headquarters. Because it was also home base to every member of Dani's team.

"You didn't have to send them, Mike. I just needed a bit of intel."

"I don't send those guys anywhere. Elizabeth and Lily just started packing and talking about shopping and maybe a trip to Disneyworld while they were on the East coast. The kids were over the moon about going on a trip."

Damon laughed quietly. "Leave it up to the ladies to make a family vacation out of it. So, what do you have for me?"

"I have a couple of doctors with some interesting secrets." The sounds of shuffling papers came through the line. "For instance, Hailey Walsh grew up in Idaho. Father is a mechanic and mother is a school teacher. In high school, Hailey got involved with a boy who would end up being the leader of a radical anti-government group. She was questioned by the local police on several occasions about him, but never gave up any useful info. Either she didn't know anything or she wasn't a snitch. The file was suppressed, since she was just a kid."

"Is she still involved with him?"

"It doesn't look like it," Mike said. "He's doing time in a Federal super-max for attempting to bomb the presidential motorcade when they came through Boise on a campaign run."

"Anything on Travis Millet?"

"He's squeaky clean, except for unexplained cash withdrawals of one thousand dollars every month."

"Any idea where the money is going?"

Mike said, "None. He doesn't have any offshore accounts or anything in his life that would lead me to believe he was being blackmailed. He pulls the money out of the ATM in two to three installments at a time. For all I know, the money is shoved under his mattress."

"Zach and Jess will find out."

"I'm still working on Claire Belgarde and Martin Graham. And as for Anuma Abenaa, you're on your own for the moment. I can't find anything on him, but that's not exactly unusual for a man born in Sierra Leone. Abenaa literally means Tuesday, and from my research it's not unusual to name an African child after the day they were born. So there are going to be a lot of Abenaas to check. I've got a call in with a friend at the embassy there, so hopefully I'll know more soon."

"Thanks, Mike. And make sure to let the guys know how much I appreciate them."

"You got it."

Damon disconnected the call. How in the world had Hailey managed to get a job with the CDC with a checkered background? And what was Travis up to? He'd focus on those two while further information was being gathered about the others.

And then he saw what he'd been watching for. Hailey. She was coming out of the motor pool and headed toward the center of camp.

Zach Steele rarely worried. The one exception was his wife—and she was safe in the hotel, probably cuddled up in bed with their five year old son, waiting for him to get back. Which he was always eager to do.

No, this worry was about his friend Damon. When Mike

Hansen called and told them a bit of what was going on, Jesse and he decided to head out and get the intel needed. Damon could handle himself better than most, but training and weapons couldn't stop a virus.

"Well, look at what I have here," Jesse Calhoun said.

He was sitting at the computer of one Dr. Martin Graham and the triumphant smile on his face raised Zach's eyebrow. "What?"

He was meticulously going through all the books on the bookshelf, looking for anything. Why folks tended to hide things in books, he'd never know, because it was always one of the first places that got checked.

"Dr. Graham has a secret numbered bank account and he's getting regular payments."

"How much?"

"Irregular amounts, but nothing over ten grand. But it's been going on for the last year, and the account has about five hundred thousand dollars in it."

Zach paused and looked at Jesse. "Sounds like a payoff of some kind."

"Enough to kill a village?"

"Who knows?" Zach looked around. The house was small but nice. The furniture was expensive but older, the paintings were prints but of well-known artists, therefore expensive. Everything was stylish and tasteful, but not luxurious. "Maybe he just wants to up his standard of living."

"Guy is anal retentive, for sure, but to kill a large amount of people for this amount of money doesn't track. If it was a million or more, I could see it, but this is small potatoes comparatively."

Zach shrugged and moved to the next bookcase. The doc had almost as many books as Zach's wife did, but his reading taste was vastly different. Live and let live. He was quick and thorough and left the computer snooping to Jesse, who was

much better and faster at it. And they'd been illegally inside
the house for only twenty minutes when Jesse scored big.

"I know what his secret is. You gotta see this shit."

Zach rounded the desk and bent over slightly to see over
Jesse's shoulder. "What the hell?"

BY THE TIME Damon got back down the hill, Hailey had
disappeared. He checked her tent, but it was empty. He
stopped a few of the soldiers passing to see if they could
point the way, but she'd apparently slipped by them as well.
Not that they'd been looking for her.

He ended up close by Travis's tent and stuck his head
inside. He was after Hailey, but it wouldn't hurt to find
Travis as well. He was about to leave when he heard the
crying. Stepping into the dark interior, he left the door ajar.
It was hot inside, as none of the flaps for the windows were
down to admit the almost nonexistent breeze.

"Hailey?"

Now the noise had moved to sobbing. He found her
wedged in between the cot/bed and a footlocker. She was
curled up in the fetal position on her side, one hand covering
her face and the other clutching a long thin metal case.

"It's Hailey, right?" he asked, as he squatted down to get a
better look at her. "I haven't had a chance to get to know you
yet."

"I'm sorry," she whispered through the sobs.

"Sorry for what?"

When he moved forward, she jerked back from him. His
eyes had adjusted to the poor light, but only her bright blond
hair gleamed in the dimness. That and the metal box in her
hands. She continued crying.

"Hailey, what's wrong?"

"I didn't know," she wailed. "Why won't he talk to me?" Then she pulled her knees further into her chest and the wail quieted to an agonizing moan. "I think I'm sick."

Damon reached out to move the hair off her face and could feel the heat coming off her skin. She was burning up. "We need to get you to sick bay."

"No," she whimpered. "I need Travis…to say sorry."

"We'll find him and tell him, okay?" He shoved the foot-locker to the side and reached for Hailey. She was small and he lifted her easily from the ground and into his arms. She curled into his body, still crying softly. Her frame was slender, almost fragile.

He carried her out of the tent and started toward the infirmary. "What's in the box, Hailey?"

"What?" She'd stopped crying, but still had her eyes closed.

"The box in your hand, what's inside?" He didn't care, but he wanted to keep her conscious and talking until he could turn her over to Dani and Dr. Nelson.

"I don't remember. It's so hot. Don't feel good…" her voice trailed off. Then she went completely limp in his arms.

He picked up his pace now that she was dead weight and he didn't have to be as careful. He cleared the infirmary door and was immediately surrounded by bio-hazard-suited nurses. One of which was Claire.

"Oh, my God," she said through the mask. "Bring her over here." She led Damon to an empty bed and he gently placed Hailey there. He turned to survey the tent. It was fully quarantined now. No one but himself and the possible Ebola victims were without masks and suits.

He saw that the two soldiers from B Company were there, and they didn't look good. Both were prone on cots, IVs hooked up to their arms and oxygen masks on. *Damn.*

Damon had hoped they wouldn't get ill, but it was spreading fast.

"This isn't normal," Claire said, unknowingly echoing Damon's thoughts. "What's happening? And how are you not sick? Dani said you carried in that private and you haven't used any protection."

"I'm not sure, but you need to be prepared for more infected. It's spreading fast." He turned to leave, and caught a glimpse of Dani. She was busy with the African man that was originally brought in. She was using a towel to wipe him down. Damon could see blood soaked bandages. There was no way that poor man was going to make it. There was just too much blood.

He felt Claire's hand on his arm and turned slightly. "You've been exposed."

Damon shrugged. "Dani already drew some blood because I'm the one that brought in Jenson over there," he nodded toward the cot that held the private first class. He was pale and clearly restless, his legs were moving under the light sheet that was covering him. He wondered if he'd ever regained consciousness. "I don't have any symptoms."

"I can't let you leave, Damon. You might be infected."

Claire had an unexpectedly strong grip, so he turned and looked at her. "I'll be fine. But right now, I need to check on Gunner."

"But you could spread the infection."

Damon gently pulled his arm away. "Take care of the girl. Since no one really knows how Ebola is spread or who will be infected, everyone in this camp has been potentially exposed. I've had close contact with two of the sick, but until their blood tests come back, we don't even know for sure if it's Ebola or not."

He could tell she wanted to argue more, so he turned her attention. "Hailey has some kind of gold case in her hands.

You might want to check it out because she had a death grip on it, even when she passed out."

They all knew it was Ebola, but his distraction worked. The doctor in her wanted everyone in a contained area for treatment, but he could see that she was curious about the case and he needed to be free to move around, so he slipped out the moment her head turned. Damon needed to know what was going on and who was behind this, before anyone died. And he was worried. Because as tough as he was, and as tough as all these Marines were, nothing could fight against a virus that killed fast and indiscriminately.

But he didn't feel sick. At all.

It didn't mean it couldn't strike at any time, but he trusted Gunner, because Gunner was a genius and because the man was determined to come up with a cure. If anyone could, Damon believed it would be his friend.

He'd check on Gunner and make sure his blood was clear. And then he needed to have a talk with the commanding officer. At this point, he would be aware of the potential risk, but Damon needed to let him know about the pet virus and the possibility of a killer in the camp. The CO was a reasonable man, but this was bound to cause a stir.

And he needed the base to be on alert for unusual activity from inside and out. And locked down. At least until he found the one responsible. Because he would, eventually.

He had a bad feeling about those rebels and that fact that Anuma was still missing. Not to mention that he'd already searched everyone's tents and belongings and had found nothing. Not one clue who was doing this or even how.

CHAPTER 11

"How is she?" Claire asked, staring down at her teammate.

Hailey was finally resting, if not comfortably, then at least not fitfully like she'd been when Damon first brought her in. Dani was sitting in a chair next to the bed, holding Hailey's pale hand with her gloved one.

"Her fever is high, but not as high as some of the others. I'm hoping that's a good sign."

Claire was tired, but when she looked at Dani, she could feel the exhaustion coming off the other woman. And she hated to bring it up, but Dani was team leader and the only person she really trusted…the only one that went out of her way to make sure they were safe.

"I found something." Her tone must have alerted Dani, even though she'd tried to keep it even.

"What did you find?"

"This," she said and handed over the long metallic box that she'd found clutched in Hailey's hand.

"What is this?"

Claire matched Dani's frown. "When Damon brought her

in, she was holding it. Wouldn't let it go until she finally went to sleep." She paused. "Look inside."

She watched Dani open the latch on the case. There were two empty syringes and a clear vial with a generic label. No way to tell what was inside. But there was a very small amount left in the very bottom. And there was a spot for a third needle that was empty. That was concerning.

"What do you think that is?"

Dani shrugged and snapped the case closed. "I don't know, but Gunner will be able to find out. Have you seen her with this case before?"

"No, but Martin has one just like it." Claire had seen him on more than one occasion with the case. "He told me that he takes vitamin B12 shots to keep his energy level up before we get deployed."

"He never said anything to me about it."

Claire doubted he would ever tell Dani about anything that might be perceived as a weakness. His ego wouldn't let him. Dani was younger and smarter than Martin and he knew it. They all knew it, which was why they chose to be on her team every time.

But all she said was, "I've never seen him with anything like that out in the field. But he had it with him in Atlanta."

She didn't know what the look on Dani's face meant, especially since her eyes were distorted behind the protective glasses. But she got up and headed toward the decontamination area, still holding the case.

Claire looked back at Hailey, who'd begun mumbling softly, twisting her legs back and forth. Even through the gloves, Claire could feel the heat coming off of her "Damn it, Hailey, what did you do?"

But the younger woman couldn't answer. And it was possible that she wouldn't ever answer again.

∾

IT TOOK ABOUT ten minutes to fully decontaminate and strip out of the biohazard suit. Dani had on khaki shorts and a tank top underneath the suit, but she was still soaked with sweat. The humidity of the area combined with the suit made working for long periods of time almost unbearable.

But bear it she would. Because she had to do her best to save as many lives as she could. She hadn't doubted her findings in the village, not really. But now she was certain. Someone on her team had turned loose a virus that was faster and more destructive than its predecessor. It was the only thing that was consistent with the data.

The question was why? None of it made any sense.

She headed for Gunner's makeshift lab with Hailey's blood for testing and the box with the vial and syringes. The tent had two sentries posted. Dani expected them to be bored with the assignment, but they looked deadly serious. Automatic machine guns were poised and ready, and they were acting vigilant.

That's when she noticed the activity. Everywhere.

The soldiers were relaxed and unarmed in the compound only this morning, merely going about their normal duties. Now, every man and woman was armed and moving with intense concentration.

"Dr. Bordeaux, you do not have access to these quarters."

One of the Marines guarding Gunner's tent had spoken, jerking her attention from the compound to his face.

He had to be mistaken. "I have blood to give to Dr. Halverson."

The other soldier inclined his head toward the command tent next door. "Dr. Halverson is in protective custody and only command staff and his escort have permission to enter."

"I don't want to push the issue, but I have to give this to

Dr. Halverson. Can you call him out here?" She paused and tried to smile. After all, she wasn't the threat. "Please?" she asked when neither of them moved.

The Marine who'd initially spoken made quick eye contact with the other one. After receiving a slight nod of assent, he entered the tent, leaving Dani outside with only one guard. It was strange to be on the outside, basically needing permission to do her job. But she could also understand the precaution. So, she waited patiently.

The soldier popped back out quickly, followed by Gunner.

"Sorry about this, Dani, but I didn't have a choice."

"Don't worry about it." Reaching out, she handed him a small cooler with everything she had. "This is Hailey's blood and something else."

Gunner accepted the cooler. "What else?"

"Hailey came in holding a metal container with two empty syringes and an unmarked vial."

He frowned as he opened the cooler. "You think it's the mutated strain?"

Dani shrugged. "What else could it be? But we won't know for sure until we can look at it under a microscope."

"There's enough to sample?"

She nodded. "Barely enough. Is there any way your watchdogs are going to let me in to help you?"

To his credit, he looked apologetic. "Your entire team is about to be quarantined, if my guess is right. Damon said the CO is scared and pissed off. That means everyone under suspicion is likely to be rounded up and interrogated."

"We don't have time for that, not with more sick people coming in." The rest of the team she could understand, but not her. At the same time, she understood the paranoia that accompanied an outbreak. And that made her think of something else. "How did our blood tests come out?"

Gunner lowered his voice because he knew what she was asking. "The three of us are showing no infection. And I took more blood from Damon about an hour ago after he brought Hailey in to the infirmary. His blood is still clear, even after two very close exposures."

"Will you be able to recreate your serum? For everyone else." She really hoped he could, because it could save lives if that was the case. The worst scenario was that the three of them were just immune for some reason, and the shots they were given didn't work, in which case there was nothing Gunner would be able to do and more people would fall ill and die.

"If I had more time and better facilities, sure. But this virus is moving so fast that we'll lose most of the camp before I can synthesize something useful."

"Damn," she said. Damon was right about her, she was a crusader, but she was also pragmatic. If she was going to be arrested and held with the others, she wanted a shower first.

"Where is Damon?" she asked.

"Hunting Travis. He seems to have found a good rock to hide under."

"He might be out of camp. As the contact tracer for our group, he normally comes and goes and no one would have thought anything of it."

"Damon is checking into that as well. Don't worry, Dani, he'll find him."

"That's what I'm worried about." Travis was no match for Damon's strength or tracking abilities. If he tried to get macho with Damon, he was going to lose more than a little pride. But she couldn't worry much about that now. She was hot, tired, and in desperate need of some soap and water.

With a quick wave, she left Gunner with the vial and headed toward her tent. It only took a couple of moments to gather up the stuff she needed for a shower plus a change of clothes. She stepped outside and ran headlong into two Marines that were clearly waiting for her.

"I need you to re-enter your tent, Ma'am."

Dani had hoped she'd get that shower, but the very serious young men standing in front of her looked like they took their orders to heart. No exceptions. But she still tried.

"I was warned that I might be detained and I will fully cooperate, but can I cooperate in the shower tent? I promise to do nothing more subversive than bathe." She made her tone light and teasing, hoping they would have a sense of humor and maybe indulge her. It wasn't like she'd be able to do anything else if they said no. They both towered over her and were armed with big scary automatic weapons.

"I'm sorry, Ma'am, but we have our orders."

She was about to give up hope when she heard his voice. The sound of reason in her suddenly messed up world. The tension unwound and she could feel her shoulders begin to relax.

"I think we can let the lady shower before making her spend a sweaty night under guard," Damon said.

He'd come up from the side, out of their vision like a shadow. His nickname was apt. Even she hadn't seen him until he'd spoken, and she should have.

"We've got our orders," they both said. Dani thought it was eerily in unison, but that was just military.

"You're orders are to keep Dr. Bordeaux contained and under guard, correct?"

They both nodded. Dani hid a smile because she knew where he was going with this.

"Then you can keep her under guard in the showers. And I will be inside myself, so I can guarantee that she won't get past me to cause you any trouble with guard duty." Then he sidestepped her watchdogs and took her hand.

The soldiers exchanged a look, shrugged, and followed along.

"I don't think those two are going to be able to be flexible enough to allow me to get my shower gear, so you're just gonna have to share, Red."

"As long as you don't mind smelling like lavender." The thought of him soaping up with her bar caused a hot tingle to start low in her belly.

"I think I'm secure enough in my manhood that I can handle some girly soap," he said.

"It's the only thing girly that I can bring when we're deployed. It reminds me of home when everything sucks."

They reached the tent and Damon pulled her inside. It wasn't a large space, but each shower cubicle was enclosed and shoulder high to help with privacy. He'd brought her to the men's shower quarters, since it was closer to her tent than the women's. He released her hand and took his shirt off while she was talking.

"I get it, and it smells nice on you."

But Dani didn't reply because she had her eyes glued to his shirtless body. She wasn't really sure what to do. She thought maybe sharing her soap meant taking turns with one of them outside. Clearly, he was planning on showering at the same time.

And Lord, he was built right. Muscles bulged in all the right places and his tanned skin was smooth enough that she wanted to glide her hands over him to see if he felt as hard as he looked.

He turned slightly and she saw his back for the first time, and the scars there caused an involuntary gasp. She stepped closer and hesitantly touched the first scar. It was a spider web of lighter colored puckered flesh, marring the perfection of his skin.

"It doesn't hurt," he said softly.

Her eyes jerked to his. He watched her intently, not moving and not stopping her from touching him. "But it must have hurt like hell when it happened," she replied.

His whole back moved up and down when he shrugged. "I lived, Doc."

She couldn't stop her hand from moving lower to another webbed ring of flesh. When Gunner had said Damon had been shot twice, it hadn't really registered for her. Logically, she understood, but right now, emotionally, she wanted to cry that he'd been in so much pain. Probably healing alone in some military hospital, not even his father knowing he was hurt. He should have had at least one person that loved him around.

"This one is so close to your spine. It could have caused paralysis or worse."

At that, he turned further so that her hand slid from his lower back to his abs. Rock hard six pack abs that contracted at her light touch. *Good Lord*, she thought, and fought the need to lick him from navel to neck—and everything in between. His scars were mostly forgotten as she willed her eyes up toward his face. She was embarrassed to be ogling his magnificent body. But she was a doctor, after all, and she admired the human form. At least, that's what she tried telling herself.

"Well, it didn't cause any paralysis. As you can plainly see."

She followed his glance downward and found his camouflage pants tighter than usual. His erection was as impressive as he was and she had to clench her hands to keep from reaching out to touch him. You'd think she never had a man the way her hormones were reacting.

"Oh," she whispered. Tearing her eyes away, she saw that he was smiling at her. And she hoped that her sudden all over body flush would be mistaken for embarrassment instead of blatant arousal. "Maybe we'd better get in the shower and cool off."

She was proud that her voice shook only a little.

Damon laughed. The sound husky and too sexual for her peace of mind. "Coward."

She stepped inside a stall and closed the curtain, refusing to fall victim to his taunt. He was too damn sexy for his own good, and she was already biased. That was the problem. Damon was her husband's twin, so she had firsthand knowledge of his anatomy, without ever touching him or seeing any more than she already had.

It was a sobering reminder. But only for her mind; her body was remembering.

"Sorry about the quarantine, Red. I tried to keep you out of it, but the CO is a hard-ass and doesn't trust anyone outside his own unit."

Dani smiled, thankful to focus on something else beside her lusty thoughts. "It's frustrating, but understandable. I would probably do the same thing in his place."

The walls were high enough that she'd have to be on a tall ladder to check out Damon's nakedness. She almost wished she had a ladder. But it broke up the sexual tension, and if she were honest with herself, she was relieved. With a side of disappointment.

Once she was stripped, she turned on the shower and had cool water streaming down over her body. She stood on tip toes to pass Damon her bar of soap. Then she heard his chuckle from the other side and wished she could see his face.

"What?" she demanded.

"I'm going to have to be careful around the guys smelling like this."

"Afraid they might get a little frisky?"

"Damn, skippy."

"Well, you do have a cute ass."

"'Bout time you noticed."

Dani shook her head as she soaped her hair. Getting clean was clearing up her head too. "Did you find Travis?"

"He's not in the camp. He skipped out this afternoon before I was able to get the perimeter locked down. And that makes him look guilty."

"He might be working—," she defended, "—And he's used to coming and going from camp."

"It's not his job at this camp. That's what Monty's team is for."

Dani didn't have an argument for that, because he was right. Even pitching in and helping was at the discretion of Dr. Nelson. Here, now, he was team leader. Even though he was with Doctors Without Borders, and not the CDC, he was a good leader.

"Need me to wash your back?" Damon asked, holding her bar of soap over the curtain. All she could see was his hand.

She laughed, "I've been washing my own back like a big girl for some time now."

"What fun is that?"

His shower turned off and he was toweling off as Dani finished soaping up her body. And if her soapy fingers lingered on her breasts just a little longer than strictly necessary for cleaning, then she couldn't be blamed. Because Damon's sexy voice and teasing tone were doing things to her that should be illegal. She wasn't even seeing anything, just listening to him talk. She heard him step out and the towel rasp across his body and she had to stop herself from peeking.

Her mouth watered at the thought of Damon, naked and still wet from his shower. Closing her eyes, she tilted her head back and rinsed her hair, half wishing Damon would go ahead and come wash her back. Her poor body, which was finally somewhat cool, revved up to broiling in an instant.

"Let's go, Red. The water's about to turn off on you."

That got her attention and she turned and rinsed off her front just as the water clicked off. She knew it was to preserve water, but Dani could have used a couple minutes more. Thankfully, Damon was dressed when she finally looked at him.

But the look on his face was more than mischievous. It was downright naughty.

"I'll be outside waiting. But hurry up, we need to discuss something important when we get back to your tent."

He was gone before Dani could say anything. She dried off and dressed in a clean tank top and shorts. What else did they need to discuss? Other than what she'd found out about Martin. Damn it, she'd been so distracted she'd forgotten to tell him about that.

She needed to tell him so they could question the other doctor about his gold case.

Dani just wanted this to end. She was lonely, overworked, and horny. Something had to give.

CHAPTER 12

*D*ani had been quiet on the short walk back to her tent. Once she was inside, Damon nodded to the two Marine guards and gave them *the look*. It was filled with all kinds of things that never needed to be spoken aloud. They backed off and set up watch more than ten feet away with an understanding nod.

He turned and went inside.

"What did you—?"

But he was on her before she could finish. His lips on hers, his hands on her, he pulled her body closer and breathed her in, the fresh lavender scent turning his brain to mush. It had been everything he could do not to rip down the flimsy curtain separating them in the shower and take her there. Instead, he'd had to wash with her damn scented soap without embarrassing himself by going off in his own hands like a teenager with his first hard-on.

"Damon," she murmured.

His tongue swept inside to taste every warm, wet part of her mouth. From her straight teeth to tangling with her own questing tongue, he wanted it all. And when her hands pulled

98

his T-shirt loose and dove underneath to touch his skin, Damon sucked in a breath.

This is what he needed. She was what he needed.

He pushed her tank top down, along with her bra straps and his hands were filled with her lush breasts as he kissed her. The sounds she made in the back of her throat urged him on. He wanted her wet and ready, but he'd dreamed about this for so long that he'd be damned if he rushed it. Even though the need to claim her was riding him hard.

Her breasts were lush as he kneaded them, nipples twin points digging into his palms. He pulled his lips from hers, kissing a path from the corner of her mouth, down her neck, only stopping to nip at her collarbone.

Her pale breasts with their soft coral tips were the most beautiful things he'd ever held. Slowly, reverently, he leaned forward and took one into his mouth. Dani gripped his shoulders, nails digging in lightly as he worshipped her. His tongue swirled and teased, and she moaned low in her throat. The moment was better than his wildest fantasy.

"I can't," she whispered. But she wasn't pushing him away.

Damon dragged his lips from her breasts, breathing heavy and trying to control the caveman inside. The one that was way past talking. And his voice was low and gravelly when he asked the question. "Tell me why."

"It's not right."

Hugging her closer, her breasts were against his chest. If only his shirt was off, then he'd be able to feel her skin against his. He let out a ragged breath. He could do this. He could talk rationally about whatever was bugging her.

"Dani," he sighed. But, deep down, he already knew. And he needed to make her see what he did. "Look at me."

"I am looking at you," she said.

He stepped back from her and tore his shirt off, even while she retreated and covered her beautiful breasts with her hands. He kept his pants on, because he wouldn't be able to think any further if he was naked with her ogling him the way she was.

"No, Dani," he said, and reached out to touch her chin. He forced her eyes up to his. "Really look at *me*. I'm not Gabriel."

When she flinched, he knew that he'd made a direct hit.

"I know that."

He shook his head. "I don't think you do. Not about this," he waved his hand between them. "Not when it counts."

"He'll always be there, Damon. Don't you see that? And you look just like him." She turned her back and he watched her shoulders round as she pulled into herself.

Damon reached out to her and pulled her back against his chest, his arms going around her body. She resisted only a moment before settling against him. But she still wouldn't look at him. So, he dealt with her ghost. Their ghost.

"You still love him?"

"I always will," she whispered.

"So do I, and I always will. You lost a husband, but I lost the other half of myself. The half that was better and brighter. And he will always be with us both."

She turned in his arms, green eyes shiny with unshed tears. "He wasn't better than you, Damon, just different."

"Exactly. Different." He brushed her wet hair out of her face. "Do I really look just like him? Every detail the same?"

He studied her while she really looked at him. Her mobile face was serious in thought and the scientist inside of her came to the surface. Every part of his face was examined visually, and then she reached up to touch him. To touch the small scar that was normally hidden by his longer hair. The one by his left ear, courtesy of some shrapnel from an I.E.D.

Her hands on his face were soft while she explored. It was a sweet kind of torture, letting her touch, while not touching.

He wanted her, but he needed her to come to him whole-heartedly, not because he was a genetic match to a dead man.

"You always wore your hair longer, didn't you? Except while you were in the Marines."

"What about my eyes, Dani?"

She turned them toward the lamp burning in the corner and put both hands on his face, her thumbs pressing lightly against his cheekbones. He briefly thought he was going to lose his mind when her breasts pressed against his chest, nipples pebbled and pointing into him. But he wouldn't break her focus.

"Your eyes are lighter than Gab..." She stopped, uncertain.

"Never be afraid to say his name. Not to me."

She nodded and exhaled the breath she'd held when she almost said his brother's name. "They're lighter and—wilder. Gabriel always said you were a daredevil, while he..."

"Was the cautious one."

Her hands slid from his face down his jaw and left his face before settling on his pecs. "What else, Dani? What else is different?"

"Your body." Her response was immediate.

He finally gave in and touched her, but only her hands. He smoothed her soft palms down his chest, and settled them on his abs. "How is it different?"

"No hair. You're smooth and hard in a way that he wasn't."

Her throat worked hard and her breathing became labored while she explored his chest and stomach. Damon was having a hard time controlling his breathing as well, and he badly wanted to explore all the curves and valleys of her body.

"I'm not Gabriel, Dani. As much as we may have looked alike, we were completely different on the inside. He studied

101

all the time and became a doctor. I barely passed high school and didn't bother with college. He was cautious and I was reckless."

He stroked her hair, liking the way the ends curled around his finger as if it didn't want to let him go. "He played fair and I don't. But I did for him. For him, I gave up the one thing I wanted."

"What was that?"

He dipped his head and gave her a quick kiss because he couldn't stop himself. "You, Dani. From the moment I saw you, I wanted you. So, I guess, in some ways we were the same. We both fell for you pretty much on sight."

"But I was already engaged to your brother."

"If it had been anyone else—anyone—I would have taken you away from him." He smiled ruefully. "But I loved my brother more than my life and he was completely, madly in love with you."

He took a deep breath, and the lavender scent mixed with her unique fragrance was making his pants even more uncomfortable. She'd stopped moving as she stared up at him, her mouth open slightly.

Not able to resist the temptation, he leaned toward her and nipped the corner. "Let me love you, Dani. I've wanted to for so long."

"I'm not sure—"

"I am," he said. "I'm not Gabriel, sugar, and I know for a fact that he wouldn't have wanted you to pack yourself away and live only on his memory." He nipped her full lower lip before using his tongue to soothe the small sting.

"I know," she said.

"Say it."

~

"You're not Gabriel," Dani said.

Damon had turned her into a boneless pile of want. His kisses drugged her mind, but he'd been right. She had been thinking of him only as a twin that genetically matched her husband. Not as his own person.

But his eyes held truth.

When she finally allowed herself to look deep into his soul, what she saw was...Damon. Not Gabriel. She'd been too much of a coward to do that before. To really look deeper into the man in front of her, instead of focusing on the similarities.

"'Bout damn time you realized it, too," he growled.

Then he kissed her again, and this time she allowed him in. The way she was going to let him into her body, she let him into her mind. And if her heart cracked open just a little, well, she'd think about that later.

Right now, she just wanted to feel. "Make love to me, Damon," she said against his lips. "Like tomorrow doesn't matter and all we have is this moment."

"I thought you'd never ask, sugar," he said, and then he put his hands on her.

They were hard, calloused hands. A working man's hands and the roughness felt so different on her softer skin. It felt good. Wild. And when he cupped her breasts and used his thumbs to scrape across her sensitive nipples, she was afraid her legs would just give out.

"You feel so good," he whispered in her ear.

Goose bumps broke out over her arms as his breath tickled that spot on her neck that drove her mad. And it was like he read her mind because he used his teeth to nibble that spot, and liquid pooled between her thighs. She couldn't stop the ragged moan that wrenched itself from her throat.

"Let's get rid of these," he said and pulled at the waist of her shorts.

Dani stepped back as he worked the buttons of the khakis. Her own hands were just as busy. She wanted to see him. To see everything that he was, because she was looking at him with new eyes. And everything about him was different than what she couldn't help but expect.

"You too," she said. "Take those off." She stepped out of her shorts as they slid down past her hips. Then her fingers were busy with the buttons of his BDU pants, but she was shaking so badly with want that she couldn't manage. His hands stopped hers.

"In a moment, I want to look at you first."

"Off now," she said it imperiously and took another step away. Then she grinned. "Doctor's orders."

The smile that broke out across his face made her stomach flutter, but it was his roguish laugh that made her clench her legs together to stop the quivering.

"Yes, Ma'am."

His long hair had fallen over his forehead as his nimble fingers went to the button of his pants. "I want you to touch yourself while I strip for you. Dip your fingers into those cute white panties and show me how wet you are."

Her face flamed at his words. It was probably the same color as her hair, but she didn't care because he looked at her like dessert. And he looked hungry. With one hand, she cupped her left breast, feeling how swollen it was, how aroused. With her right hand, she skimmed her waist and paused only briefly at the waist of her panties before dipping inside.

"Just like that. Tell me what you feel, Dani. Tell me what I do to you," he said, while he undid the button of his pants and slid them carefully over his large erection.

Dani touched herself, feeling the heat and slick wetness that greeted her fingers. But it wasn't her finger she wanted there, she wanted all the hardness that was being unveiled to her as Damon stepped out of his pants and hooked his thumbs into the waist of his underwear.

His voice was low and husky and he hadn't moved toward her again. "Tell me."

"You get me hot," she said it simply. Because it was a raw feeling. She moved her fingers along the outside of her labia before exploring deeper, touching her inner lips. "My fingers aren't enough. You did that, Damon. You make me burn inside."

"Goddamn, you're beautiful. Take those panties off. I want to see for myself how wet you are."

Dani hooked her left thumb into the side of her panties, and pulled them down an inch before she stopped. She left her right hand inside, still touching herself. She'd never done anything like this before and just his eyes and words were about to make her come. It was like she was on display for his pleasure—and hers—and it felt naughty.

"You too," she said, nodding at him and looking pointedly at the part of him that she desperately wanted to feel. With her hands and with her mouth. It had been so long since she'd allowed anyone close, and it had been eight long years since she'd made love. She reached out, showing him her glistening fingers.

His boxer-briefs hit the floor at the same time as her panties. He groaned.

She reached for him and he was there. Their lips met and bodies melded and Dani was overwhelmed with the sensations. His hard chest rubbed her breasts and his big hands cupped her butt, lifting her to meet his hungry mouth.

He kissed her like a man savoring the most expensive champagne.

"I want you, Damon." She had to say his name aloud. Otherwise, she might decide this was a just a lust-filled dream. One that, if she were honest, she'd had before.

"I need to be inside you."

"Yes," she moaned.

He picked her up and she wrapped her legs around him. His hardness hitting her in the most sensitive place and almost sending her over the edge. She had to bite her lip to stop from letting go. She licked his neck and bit his earlobe. He tasted salty and smelled of her soap. It was a heady combination.

"Fuck, baby. You're making my knees weak."

He had her blanket down on the ground with her pillow while he still held her, but then he was on his knees laying her on her back and she reached out to stroke his shaft. He bucked in her hands and sucked in a breath. But he stayed on his knees feasting on her with his gaze.

"That's the idea, sugar," she drawled.

The look in his eyes went a little feral when she imitated his Louisiana drawl, and suddenly his hands were every-where. He touched, kneaded, and stroked her into a frenzy. His hands were between her legs, fingers on her, before sliding inside. Her back arched in pleasure and she closed her eyes.

"Look at me." His voice was gruff but insistent.

Her eyes popped open and she was seared by his look. "Damon—"

The condom in his hand seemingly appeared from nowhere, but she knew they were readily available on the base. He sheathed himself and shifted off of his knees, coming down between her thighs. He supported his weight on his elbows as he tangled his fingers in her hair.

"You're beautiful, Red."

Dani had her hands on his biceps, loving the hard strength she found there. "Make me yours," she whispered.

And he did. Inch by hard inch, he slid inside her slick channel, stretching unused muscles with his size and kicking her into an orgasm as soon as he was seated to the hilt. And it was everything she'd missed about sex. Rockets and stars and blindness to everything but the feelings she was experiencing.

"So good. Oh, my God."

Damon kissed her, stealing what little breath she had. "You feel incredible," he said.

And when he moved, he took her the way a pirate takes gold. Forcefully, and with not a shred of hesitancy that a new lover might have. She loved it. Loved that he lost control and pinned her to the floor, taking her in a way that she'd never been taken before. She felt claimed as he surged in and out of her.

There were no more words left, just this blinding need to be one with this man.

Her body matched his rhythm and her hips rose eagerly to meet each demanding thrust, her passion rising beyond anything she'd ever known. His hands were twined with hers, holding them above her head. He kissed her wildly, tongue moving in time with his hips, stealing her moans.

Dani wrapped her legs around his waist and squeezed, using her inner muscles to bring them both more pleasure. And when she peaked for the second time, she could feel her inner contractions setting off Damon's orgasm.

His body shuddered as he slowed his thrusts. And he kissed her so tenderly that tears came to her eyes.

Damon rubbed his nose against hers. "That was incredible. You get me so damn hot for you. Next time it'll be slower, and by the time I'm done with you, I'll have tasted every single inch of you."

"I think maybe I've already died from pleasure."

"I know I did."

Dani wiggled when she realized that something was digging into her shoulder. "Why are we on the ground?" She only just then realized they weren't on her cot. The man was dangerous to a woman's state of mind.

"Your bed wasn't sturdy enough for us. For this."

She laughed hard and shook her head. She was a respected doctor, for cripes' sake, not some simple farm girl who just lost her virginity while in a haze of lust. Okay, maybe she'd been in a haze, but Dani should have noticed.

Damon smiled down at her. "I love to hear that laugh, and I have a feeling that you don't let it out often enough. Life is too short."

"There hasn't been much to laugh about for a long time."

Damon brushed his thumb across her cheek and stroked her hair. "About that. I'm a little worried about your God complex."

She knew her brow was furrowed as she frowned. "What God complex? That's more Martin's style."

He shook his head. "Gabriel died from Hemorrhagic Fever, Dani."

She avoided his eyes. She knew what he was talking about and she should've kept her damn mouth shut. "I know that."

"There was no way, short of an actual Bible school miracle, that you could have saved him. You need to let it go. Let him go."

What she might have said was lost as a loud booming noise echoed through the camp. It vibrated through her like a beat from a loud bass stereo. Dani was slow to react because she didn't recognize the sound, but Damon was immediately on his feet and had his pants on faster than she could even process what was happening.

"Shadow?" It was the voice of one of the Marines guarding her tent. He sounded tense.

Damon answered. "Stand fast, soldier. I'm on my way."

"Copy that."

"What was that?" Dani asked.

"Sounded like an RPG." He reached down and pulled her up from the blanket on the floor. He gave her a quick kiss, but he was clearly already thinking about what might be going on. "Get dressed and stay here. I need to find out what's happening."

Not bothering with the clothes, Dani framed her hands on either side of his face and pulled his gaze to hers. "You be careful."

"WETSU." He winked at her. "We-Eat-This-Shit-Up," he answered to the question she'd been about to ask. "This is what I do, sugar."

And then he was gone.

"That's what I'm afraid of," she whispered.

CHAPTER 13

amon made a quick stop at his tent to grab some gear and his sniper rifle. Then he headed toward the front of the camp. That's where Gunner was, and it was where the concussive sound of the grenade had come from.

"'Bout time you got here," Gunner said. He was outside with one guard and a pair of binoculars.

Damon dropped his pack and started checking his rifle, loading it, and making sure the safety was on. Semi-automatic weapon fire sounded in the distance, and he could just barely make out the sounds of an engine straining. Someone was driving toward them, and pushing the vehicle past what it could normally handle. He didn't bother to look; he just listened.

"What can you see?" he asked.

Gunner grunted. "Not a goddamn thing." There was a long pause and then he said, "Got it. Two vehicles coming straight for us. The front truck is swerving and taking fire from the one behind."

"How long?"

"Three minutes. Max."

The radio crackled and the Marine standing guard answered his handheld. He had the volume too low to hear, but he copied the message and turned to them. "CO wants Dr. Halverson in the command tent and wants you on that hill on overwatch." He pointed toward the hill that Damon had claimed for his private phone calls.

"Got it."

He slung his rifle across his back again and picked up his bag. He was at a dead run and on that hill in about a minute and a half. He dropped to a knee and began setting up his spot while he caught his breath. The whole camp had mobilized, and anyone not sick was either on guard duty or at the perimeter ready for whatever was headed their way.

Damon had a portable radio with him, and as he plugged in the ear piece, he could hear excited chatter from the Marines at the entrance to the camp. They had night vision and were giving an update on the incoming possible combatants. Vehicle one was on older model small truck that was still taking fire and occupied by at least two males, maybe a third. There seemed to be some confusion on that point.

Vehicle number two was a Jeep. There were four heavily armed males inside, and only the driver wasn't firing. Damon listened to all of it while he set his rifle up on its stand and began adjusting his scope to night vision. All the while, he was slowing his heart rate by breathing in and out in the controlled way he'd been taught so long ago. It was second nature to him at this point.

"Shadow, you copy?"

"Copy," he answered.

"Report."

He focused and the truck came into his sights. He recognized Travis immediately. He was the driver. The man in the passenger seat was almost unrecognizable as a human being, his face was so badly beaten. But he was African and there was an African child in the middle. His head bobbed up and down with the force of the truck driving over the uneven terrain.

"Vehicle one is non-combatant. Take out number two."

"Copy that."

Damon knew there was one other sniper in B Company that was very capable, and it was his job to stop that Jeep. So Damon focused on the landscape. There was no way they were alone.

He didn't hear the shot, but the Jeep swerved violently to the left as the driver slumped over the wheel. The two males standing in the back shooting didn't have a chance to hold on before they were flung out like rag dolls. The passenger was in better shape until the Jeep bucked up and flipped over on its side. Damon could only see a cloud of dust and the spinning wheels of the undercarriage.

Travis had made it to the front gates, where he was getting out of the truck, hands high in the air. Damon thought the passenger looked like Anuma, but he still couldn't be sure. He was slumped over against the door.

Damon scanned the tree line. And he picked up movement. A lot of movement.

"We've got more company," he said into his radio.

"How many?" The voice in his ear was from the command tent. Another radio operator like Private Jensen.

"Fifty, give or take," he answered. "Ragtag group, but some have on uniforms. All armed."

"We had intel about some rebel activity moving our way." There was a long pause as options were discussed and discarded. Most of which he wouldn't be privy to. Then the order came. "Stand fast."

Damon was used to waiting. "Copy that." And the larger

group had stopped out of range. Most were using the trees as cover still. They were being smart.

At the gates, Travis was taken into custody and the man Damon thought was Anuma was pulled out of the truck, his body limp. Beside him was a boy of about seven or eight. The child's ebony skin gleamed in the moonlight and Damon could see him clutching Anuma's limp hand like a lifeline.

What the hell was Travis up to? And what was Anuma involved in? Because he had no doubt that the men following them were the same as the ones that attacked Dani's camp in Ghana. That they'd found Dani's group again all the way in Liberia meant something important. But what, Damon would have to wait to find out.

Anuma looked out of commission, but Travis was still upright and looked relatively unharmed. He'd better be a straight arrow with some answers. Otherwise, Damon would take pleasure in beating them out of him.

He was still watching the tree line when his SAT phone rang.

DANI'S HEART was lodged somewhere in her throat as the gunfire got closer. Not being able to see anything was driving her crazy. But when she stuck her head outside to ask for information, she'd been politely, but firmly, told to get back inside.

And she wasn't about to argue with her guards.

She just hoped Damon was okay, even though she knew that out of everyone, he should be fine, since he'd be up high somewhere watching over the Marines on the ground. That's what he did. He was a protector. Always had been. But that didn't stop her from wringing her hands together in worry.

With her imagination out of control, she focused instead

113

on what had just taken place between them. And how Damon made her feel. Free and out of control. Which was a completely different experience from what she'd shared with Gabriel. With Gabe, it was about a mutual sharing, minds and hearts. He'd been a gentle lover, if unimaginative, loving her mind as well as her body. Their shared loved of medicine and helping others became a passion that surpassed mere physical sensation. She'd often wondered if he'd loved her mind more than her body.

But not with Damon.

With him, it was a taking. She felt robbed of sanity, able to focus only on the feelings he invoked. And she took as well. Took his control. Dani loved that she was able to make him as crazy as he made her, as wild to join, to meld in a way that she'd never experienced. Twins, but so different fundamentally that it was impossible to hold onto her anxiety over hurting Damon by using him to relive the past.

Because she wasn't.

Dani was forging a new path, with a new partner. Someone who wanted her body. It was heady to be wanted as a desirable woman first, instead of primarily respected for her intelligence. And she'd been missing that, even if she hadn't realized it. As a fertile female in her prime, her body wanted and needed satiation, but her head had been slow to catch on.

She needed to turn her darned mind off and just listen to her body.

"Ma'am."

Dani lifted her head and found her guard at the opened door. "What happened?"

"I need to move you to a different location."

She got to her feet instantly. "Where are we going?"

"You're going to the infirmary, Ma'am." Then he fell in

behind her as she moved out of her tent and headed in the direction he wanted.

She wasn't sure why the change, but she'd be a damn sight more useful helping out somewhere else, rather than being cooped up alone in her tent. "Just Dani is fine with me."

He didn't answer, but she was already distracted by Martin, who was not complying with his own guard. "I demand to be taken to the commanding officer right this instant."

"Save it, Doc. He's got bigger things to deal with than whatever crawled up your narrow ass."

Dani couldn't hear anymore gunfire, but that didn't mean it was over. "Just go inside, Martin."

"I'm a respected doctor—"

She sighed and grabbed his elbow, cutting him off before he could really get going. "I know, but there's something bigger going on here than your ego, so can you put it away for a moment and just cooperate, please?"

Dani dragged Martin inside the infirmary. This was the non-quarantined tent, and was almost completely empty except for a small group in the corner. "Travis," she called out. "Where have you been?"

He looked up at her in surprise, but then his faced closed down. "I went looking for Anuma."

Dani and Martin moved closer, one guard staying just inside the tent and another standing outside. When Travis stood, she had a clear view of Anuma. He was lying prone on a cot. His breathing was shallow and his face was so badly bruised that his eyes were swollen shut.

"My God. What happened?" she asked, as she rushed over to check out his injuries. Martin was uncharacteristically silent as he took up position on the opposite side.

Even though they were often at odds, Martin was a consummate professional when it came to medicine and he began assessing injuries, calling out softly what he found, just as Dani was. Then he moved away to get some supplies. Besides the numerous contusions over his body, Anuma had several broken ribs, which was causing the difficulty breathing. Travis had moved over to a corner, out of the way. Only a couple of other patients were occupying the tent, but they stayed silent.

Dani was about to begin removing Anuma's dirty and torn clothing so they could clean him up when a small head and huge eyes peeked up at her from somewhere under the cot. The eyes were near Anuma's head, but she couldn't see the rest of the child's body.

She lowered her voice, "Hello, there."

"Hello." His little voice was heavily accented.

"Are you Anuma's friend?" Dani knelt down to get on eye level, but didn't move closer. It was obvious the little guy was scared, but he gave her a tentative smile, showcasing a couple of missing teeth. When he nodded, Dani smiled. "He's my friend too."

"Doctor?"

"Yes. I want to help your friend. Would you like to help me?"

The smile widened and the child scooted out front under the cot, standing up, but still keeping a little distance between himself and everyone else. He was about seven or eight years old, his head was shaved, and his clothing was too big for his little frame.

What a cutie, she thought. "What's your name?"

He shot a quick look at Travis before answering. "Frankie."

That caught her off-guard, since it was a fairly unusual name and not in the least tribal. But she rolled with it. "Can you do me a favor, Frankie?"

He nodded solemnly.

116

"I need you to hold Anuma's hand for me while we clean him up and put some bandages on him. It's going to hurt, and I think he'd feel better if you were holding onto him. Can you do that?"

He nodded again and stepped forward to Dani's side. She moved out of the way to let him close to the cot. "Thank you, Frankie."

"Travis? Martin and I could use your help here," Dani said, as she prepared to take off Anuma's shirt.

When he didn't move, she glanced up at him to see him staring at the boy. He had the most peculiar look on his face before he shrugged and moved to help. With his help, they were able to strip the tattered, dirty shirt off. Then they worked on the pants. Once Anuma was cleaned up, Dani began assessing the injuries.

"Looks like the worst of it is the broken ribs. The rest are bruises and minor cuts." Martin kept quiet while he worked and Travis was unusually silent as well. "What happened to him?"

"Yes, Travis, why don't you enlighten all of us," Damon's voice cut across the tent.

Dani couldn't help the feeling of safety and comfort that wrapped around her at his presence. She shook her head. This was pathetic, but she didn't care. He made her happy in a way that couldn't be stopped. Not even during some kind of threat hanging over them outside, as well as the Ebola threat inside the camp.

Travis glanced at the boy again. The child was sitting quietly next to the cot at Dani's feet, holding onto Anuma's hand. His face was solemn, and unlike Travis, his face gave nothing away.

"I don't see how it's any of your business," Travis said. His tone was quiet but belligerent.

Damon stalked forward. His shirt and knees were

covered in dirt and Dani guessed that he'd been lying on his stomach on the hill, covering the front of the camp with his rifle. His face was set and grim, and even though he barely glanced at her, she felt the brief look all the way down to her toes.

"It's my business because the rebel leader outside is demanding we give you to them for quote, 'crimes against their tribe.' So, you'd better say something before I drag your ass to the commander to let him decide what to do with you." Damon was close enough to grab Travis, and Dani could see he was fighting the urge to step back, away from the obvious threat.

Travis puffed up, "I'm an American citizen, and a doctor, and you can't just hand me over to them."

"So am I, and I'd like to know why I'm in danger because of you." That came from Martin and it surprised Dani because he said it quietly, without all the pomp he would normally infuse his voice with. That, more than anything, told her that he was very worried.

"Tell them."

Dani spun back to Anuma when he spoke. It was barely a whisper, but in the sudden silence it was heard clearly. Anuma was awake and staring at Travis with his right eye, the one not swollen shut and turning purple.

"Tell them," he repeated through cracked and bloody lips. When he attempted to sit up, Dani touched his shoulder and firmly kept him on his back.

"You have several broken ribs. You need to keep still," she said. Then she focused on the man everyone else was staring at. "And you need to tell us what's going on. Now."

His eyes pleaded with her, but whatever his secret was, it was putting them all in danger. Then, he dragged in a ragged breath and moved closer to Anuma. Whatever he saw in the other man's battered face must have convinced him to talk.

"Frankie is my son," Travis said.

Dani wasn't sure what she expected, but it wasn't even close to that statement. She looked down at Frankie. How had this happened and how had no one on the team known? One look at Martin's face showed the same kind of shock she was feeling.

"How is did this even happen? You know we're prohibited from being involved with the villagers in that way," Dani said. She looked down at the child. "Frankie, how old are you?"

"Eight summers."

Dani smiled at the boy before swinging incredulous eyes toward her contact tracer. Clearly, he'd been doing more than tracking down families infected with Ebola. He hung his head and his shoulders dropped. Stepping back and away from Damon, Travis sat down on a nearby cot, as if the burden of this was too much to bear.

She'd only been working with Travis for the last five years, and before that he'd been with Doctors Without Borders. Frankie obviously took after his mother, because she couldn't see any of Travis in his little face. And while he seemed to accept and understand what Travis said, he was clinging to Anuma, not his father. "What happened?"

Damon had moved away to speak with the guard stationed inside the tent, and while she was aware of him on a deeper level, she was focused on the man before her. The one who suddenly looked a lot older than his twenty-eight years.

"I was young, dumb, and infatuated with being a savior." He scraped a hand down his face, smearing dirt and wiping some off. "The chief's daughter was already a widow, and when she snuck into my tent the first time, I thought she was just looking for a little fun. It was forbidden, for both of us, and maybe that's what made it seem so exciting. So taboo. I don't have any excuses and it was my fault. I should have sent her away and saved us both."

"But you got her pregnant instead," Martin said it, heavy censure hanging in the air between them all.

Dani agreed, but didn't want to say it in front of the boy. Frankie was a quiet kid, but that didn't mean he wasn't sensitive.

Travis nodded. "I didn't even know about it. By the time I found out, she'd died in childbirth and Anuma was sent to find me."

Dani was confused. "How is Anuma involved in this?"

But it was the battered man on the cot that answered her. "The girl was my sister."

"What do the men outside this camp want with you, Travis?" Damon asked.

For a moment, it didn't look like Travis would answer. He stared at Dani, his look apologetic. "The leader of that group is Anuma's father. He found out that I was back and he wants me dead, even though I've been sending money for the care of Frankie and their village. He still blames me for the death of his daughter. Anuma was taking the boy away from the old man, because he'd begun to be abusive to him. Because of me."

Dani gasped. "Is he the one responsible for this?" she asked, pointing toward all the bruises and swelling covering Anuma's body. When Travis nodded, Dani could only shake her head. Then she turned to Anuma. "Why did you set that village on fire?"

Anuma coughed, the movement painful and causing his face to twist. When his breathing returned to what it was, he answered. "My father punished that village by contaminating it with poison. I've seen it before. I could not allow them to return, only to have more die. Better they lose everything and rebuild."

"But he saved something for you, Dani," Travis said. "It's inside the truck. Maybe you can have your watchdog get it for you."

Dani ignored the bitterness. Damon didn't care what Travis said, but she wanted to know what Anuma had, and she felt such relief that he'd set that fire to help those people, not cause them further harm. Because he was right, losing valuables and housing was better than death.

"What is it?"

"It's all of your samples from the village. He pulled it out of your tent before he set the fire and hid it in the jungle in case his father's rebels caught him. Which they did."

Damon spoke up from beside her. She hadn't even heard him move. He stroked a finger down her back in a small caress that everyone saw, but she didn't care. "I'll get the case, Dani. But first, Travis needs to have a little chat with the CO."

"He won't really be turned over to them, will he?" Dani didn't want Travis dead. Seriously reprimanded—sure—but not physically in danger.

"No, he's an American, and we don't deal with terrorists. Ever."

Travis wouldn't make eye contact with her as Damon escorted him out of the tent, and that was fine with her. He'd violated ethical rules that she held sacred, while hiding a love child and paying money to him, but not stepping up and really caring for him the way a father should. Dani had lost all respect for the man she thought was a friend and a decent human being, especially since Frankie had been suffering abuse because of who his father was.

The child was sound asleep on the floor under Anuma's cot. He was curled up, knees tucked into his chest, his sweet round face slack with exhaustion.

Dani ran her hands through her hair and looked up to

find Martin staring at her. "You don't have any secrets you've kept from everyone, do you?" Her voice was hard, but she was only kidding.

His half smile looked mocking. "Actually, I do."

And that's when the world exploded.

CHAPTER 14

*B*etween the screaming and the gunfire, Damon could barely hear himself breathe. He and Travis were thrown to the ground after several rounds landed. The rebels had been hiding more than themselves in the trees. They'd been hiding a couple of damn rocket launchers. The really old kind, probably sold off when the newer more advanced models became available. That chief wanted Travis dead, and he obviously didn't care if he took everyone else with him, including his grandson.

They managed to hit both the medical tents and one of the personnel tents in the center of camp. The screaming was coming from the quarantine area, where the Ebola patients were being treated. Marine personnel were running in that direction.

"What was that?" Travis choked out.

"SMAW." Damon was up on his feet, already focused on the collapsed tent that was smoking. The tent he had just been inside with Dani. He reached down and jerked Travis to his feet.

"What does that even mean?"

Damon tugged him along, even though his own legs were a bit shaky. "Shoulder-launched Multipurpose Assault Weapon," he threw over his shoulder. "Now, shut up and help me find Dani." The tent supports were leaning in, forming a weird looking sunken teepee-type structure. Damon reached the door and ripped it the rest of the way off its hinges. "Dani," he yelled inside. The gunfire going on just outside of the camp made hearing anything more difficult. When he heard nothing, he started lifting canvas to let light in.

"Grab something to support this," he said to Travis. "Dani! Goddamn it, answer me."

Instead of moving, Travis ducked under Damon's arms and stood, supporting the heavy canvas over his head. "Get them out."

He didn't waste any time. Diving inside, he felt his way until he touched something warm. It was an arm, but it was too small to be Dani's. He tugged and was able to pull the limp body of the little boy, Frankie, from the folds of the tent.

"Dani," he said again. "Can you hear me?"

"I think everyone can hear you yelling," Martin's answer came muffled from somewhere inside.

"Are you all okay?"

"If you mean Danielle, yes, she's going to be fine. She's unconscious because she threw herself over Anuma when the place caved in. But her vitals are good. I'm fine too, thanks for worrying."

"Let me get Frankie out and I'll be back for you," Damon said, ignoring the doctor. He had to fight the urge to keep going forward until he found Dani, but he was going to trust Martin that she would be fine. He needed to get the child to safety.

Struggling out of the tight confines of the ruined infirmary, he found several more Marines and Claire. She was wringing her hands and tears streaked down her face. Blood matted one side of her head, but otherwise she looked relatively unharmed.

"What about Dani?" she asked.

"I'm going back in for her."

"Get her out."

She was borderline hysterical, breathing rapidly through her mouth. It looked like she might grab him, but resisted the urge. There was something going on in her expression that he couldn't decipher, and she was sweating profusely. The soldiers were busy rigging the canvas to pull it up and out, so they could get everyone else outside. The gunfire was now only sporadic. He hoped Gunner was safe, but couldn't worry about it now.

He was needed here.

And he needed to see her—with his own eyes—to make sure she was fine. Until he held that woman in his arms, he wouldn't stop. He handed Travis his son, grabbed a flashlight from one of the men, and turned to plunge inside again. The canvas was heavy and cumbersome to move through, but with the soldiers outside working to prop up and pull poles back into place, it was becoming easier to see.

"It's about time, Shadow," she said, voice raspy.

Damon's knees almost gave way when he saw her, hair sticking up in all directions and dirt dusting her bright head. He looked her up and down, seeing no injuries. He relaxed slightly, but he wouldn't be happy until she was out of this mess and back in his arms.

"Sorry, Red. Won't happen again."

Martin looked no worse for the collapse, but Anuma was no longer awake, and his breathing was even worse than before. Dani saw his concern and answered the unspoken question. "The roof landed on us and I couldn't stop it from hitting him. We've got to get an X-ray to make sure a rib hasn't punctured his lungs."

Damon could see that the side of the tent that had been hit was blackened and smoldering, now that it was lifted slightly. The smoke and burned canvas smell was acrid and stung his eyes. "Help me with this pole, Martin."

The doctor nodded and they both grasped the pole that was lying over on its side, but lifted from whatever the soldiers outside were doing. If he and Martin could lift it up to prop some of the canvas aside, they'd have a clear path to get out and get a stretcher or gurney inside for Anuma. From the looks of him, moving him without help might do more harm than getting him out right away.

"I'll get someone to bring a stretcher," Dani said, as she skirted around the cot and headed toward the light she could see.

When Dani was out of sight, Damon set his flashlight aside to illuminate the space, and then worked with Martin to hold the one intact support beam up. There was nothing to prop it up with, so they were just going to have to hold it until the soldiers outside could get in and get everyone else out. He didn't have much hope for the other side of the room. That was where it looked like a bomb had exploded, and the two sick men there were likely dead.

"Did you know about Travis's little secret?" Damon asked.

"I had no idea, but that is the kind of thing that will ruin his reputation and get him fired from the CDC."

"So, what's your little secret, Doc?"

Damon was up close, watching Martin's expressions as well as he could in the semi-dark. The light from the small opening he'd come through was getting brighter and he could hear the conversations going on outside as men worked on the supports to get that stretcher inside.

"What are you talking about?" he said, sounding bored.

But he looked away and blinked several times. It was as good as any poker tell.

"I mean those deposits into that numbered account that have been getting bigger. And the fact that someone is mutating the Ebola virus. Someone from your team, Doc."

"You must have some good people looking into my affairs to find that."

He didn't blink this time or look away. He didn't even sputter about the numbered account they'd found that was damned hard to find because it wasn't in his name. For the current situation, that looked suspicious as hell. And Damon had been ready for outrage and denial. He'd positioned his body in a way that he could grab his gun or knife if he needed to, but he didn't think Martin was involved. Oh, he was hiding something, but it wasn't the virus.

And his next words confirmed Damon's suspicions.

"I thought something was going on in that village, but Dr. Bordeaux was keeping all the samples to herself, which was odd." He paused for a moment, clearly thinking. "Why didn't I catch this sooner?"

"Where is the money coming from, Martin? Are you getting paid to mutate this virus?"

The man actually smiled. Damon thought it was the first time he'd actually seen teeth. His normal expression was a scowl or a smirk.

"I can assure you that I'd never, ever, infect anyone with a deadly virus on purpose. I do take my Hippocratic Oath seriously. Nor do I have the finesse to mutate one."

"You strike me as the kind of man who thinks he can do anything, just to prove he can." Damon prodded him, hoping to see some sign of guilt. But it just wasn't there. He looked genuinely concerned and he wasn't running away from the conversation.

Martin shrugged. "Contrary to popular opinion, I do

know my limitations. I may not like to admit them, but I do know them."

"Then, explain the money. It makes you look guilty of something. Why else hide it?"

The support moved suddenly, and both men scrambled to keep it steady. Damon could hear an engine outside, so they must have a truck or rhino outside moving debris. Someone yelled inside that they almost had it.

"Just get the fucking stretcher in here," Damon yelled back. "We don't have all day." Then he looked back at the doctor. "The money?"

"It's a secret because it will irreparably damage my reputation."

"Everyone thinks you're a narcissistic prick. How much worse can it be?"

"Hell," he said. "Might as well tell someone, since this mutated Ebola virus will likely kill us all anyway as fast as its spreading." He let out a long sigh and then just shook his head. "I've been in contact with a journalist, who has been paying me for dirt on the CDC, as well as some other agencies that I've been involved with."

Damon thought he said it like he just confessed to having an unchecked case of genital warts. "So?"

"So—With Ebola being the new big scary thing for the uninformed public, the large news stations are paying for information. The kind that hurts the government..."

Of all the things he could have said, that one actually surprised Damon. They'd obviously strung up a brighter light outside because the room was a little brighter as the canvas slowly began rising. He and Martin let go of the support as it too rose, attached to the roof as it was, and Damon flexed his shoulders, keeping an eye on the doctor.

"No shit? You're a whistle blower?"

Martin puffed up a little. "I believe that the public has

the right to know how very little our government is actually investing in their welfare. Even more, I've been contracted to write an exposé about the FDA and how they decide to dole out cures for common illnesses or not, depending on how much money could be made in their deals with the big pharmaceutical companies. Big Pharma don't want cures; they want to sell drugs. New drugs that are too expensive, but line their execs' pockets, while people suffer and die…"

"And here I thought Dani was the only crusader. Who's your contact?"

"You're not going to let this go, are you?"

Damon shook his head. "Doc, I'll tell everyone I know in the government about your deal and let you deal with the fallout, unless you come clean and let me check out your story."

"Krystal Cummings is her name. And she's a bit more than just a contact."

"So, you're screwing the journalist that's planning on screwing the government? Is that about the size of it, Doc?"

"Yes. As crass as you put it, that is what's going on, and if it all comes out before we're ready, then *I'm* screwed. My reputation will be shot, I'll be fired, and with the Patriot Act in place, probably taken someplace horrible and interrogated."

Damon shook his head. "Don't get all melodramatic."

Several soldiers ducked under the remaining canvas that was still hanging low. "You two okay?"

Damon pointed at the cot where Anuma was still unconscious and wheezing badly. "He needs medical attention now."

The Marine nodded and turned to shout out orders. Martin turned the topic and Damon let him. "Travis is a doctor in the basic sense, but he does most of our contact

129

tracing, almost exclusively. And, clearly, he and Anuma have been in collusion about this love child thing."

Damon nodded as the stretcher finally made it inside. But Dani wasn't with it. It only worried him for a moment as Martin talked through the problem, now that he knew about it. And Damon was convinced that he'd been in the dark about it. His story about the journalist made a lot of sense, and having his name in the headlines would appeal to his ego. His eyes were steady and grim as he considered the implications of the current infection.

"You clearly thought I was a suspect, which means that Dani has something definitive in the way of proof. And she would never do something like this, so she's off the suspect list."

This wasn't news to Damon, who nodded toward the entrance and started walking after the men who had Anuma on the stretcher. Martin continued, "Hailey is young. She doesn't have the patience to do test after test. And that's what it would take to mutate a virus that is already a perfect killer, not to mention she is a freshman member of the team and wouldn't have access to the necessary supplies."

"That leaves Claire," Damon said, grimly.

Martin nodded. "She has the patience and maturity, as well as a background in genetics. But, would she?"

"Where in the hell is Dani? She's supposed to be right here."

Damon searched through the small crowd and didn't see either of the women. Claire had been standing right outside, wringing her hands, the last time he'd seen her. Damn it, he should have seriously considered her earlier instead of focusing on getting the truth out of Martin or Travis. Zach and Jesse had found the money trail, and Damon had thought it might be him. It would explain the large amounts of money coming in on a monthly basis.

Claire had stayed on his periphery, maybe because Dani trusted her and his friends hadn't been able to find anything discriminating against her. Nothing. No strange bank accounts, no mad scientist lab equipment in her apartment, just nothing.

Her apartment was too clean. Jesse had called it sterile. Impersonal to a point, as if someone had decorated it for her and she rarely spent time there. No family photos either, that's what Zach had said, and he thought it was weird because she came from a large family.

"What would Claire have to gain?"

Martin shrugged. He looked at a loss. "She lives for the work. Why would she put her own life in jeopardy to do this?"

"It's more complicated than that," Gunner said, coming into the conversation.

Damon no longer heard gunfire, just the sounds of clean-up going on in various areas of the camp. "What happened with the rebels?"

"Our guys kicked their asses, probably all the way back to Sierra Leone by now," Gunner said. His escort was two steps behind him and muttered "get some" to Gunner's statement. "But I have more information about what's going on."

Damon had asked several of the soldiers if they'd seen Dani or Claire, but in the confusion of getting the big tent propped up, but no one remembered seeing where they went. It didn't matter; Damon would tear the whole fucking place apart if he needed to. He would find Dani.

"What do you know, Gun?"

"You weren't answering your SAT phone," he nodded toward the tent, "Clearly, you were busy. So, your buddy Zach called me and told me a strange little story about a woman and her obsession."

"Claire?"

Gunner nodded. "Yep."

Damon was almost afraid to ask, but Martin wasn't as he jumped in. "What obsession?"

"Dani," Gunner said. He still had the SAT phone in his hand. "Claire has a little house outside the city that was an inheritance from a grandmother. It's not even in her name, which is why no one knew about it. She's got a small, but very expensive, lab set up in one of the rooms, but it's the rest of the house that's the real problem."

"Just spit it out, Goddammit." Damon was beginning to pace as he listened, his mind swirling. He needed to be doing something other than standing there listening to Gunner. Dani was in serious danger and his gut was screaming at him to move. But he forced himself to stay and listen.

"The whole fucking place is a shrine to Dani." Gunner reached out and grabbed Damon's shoulder, to stop the pacing. "Life size pictures of her everywhere, poetry, letters about how much Claire loves her. Zach said it's creepy as fuck."

"But how does mutating the virus fit into her obsession?"

Martin was the one that answered. "I think I know."

Damon glanced at Gunner and they both turned to look at the doctor.

"The CDC is getting the virus under control, which means no more deployments. Dani is more valuable and sought after in Atlanta, so our team was going to be split up. We found out right before we deployed this last time. Dani was stepping down as team leader to work full time at head-quarters. Claire would have been reallocated to another division. If what your friend found is true—"

"Then Claire would need a reason to keep Dani in a position to be deployed with her." Damon was a damned fool. He should have seen it, somehow.

Gunner started cussing. "She killed that village to stay

closer to Dani, to make sure that Dani would continue her mission to save the whole fucking world."

"Obsession," Damon said it under his breath. "Dani's got a savior complex and Claire knows it because they've been best friends for years."

"More than that, man," Gunner said. "She's pissed off. At you. I saw the way she looked at you and I couldn't figure out where all that hostility was coming from."

"What the fuck are you talking about?"

"You never saw it, because you never took your eyes off of Dani, but it was there. I thought she was just worried you were going to take advantage of her friend or something. But now I think it was jealousy. That's why we had an outbreak here again. I think Claire is trying to kill you."

"Why not just infect me directly then? Why start with Private Jensen?"

Martin answered. "She's smart enough to try to hide her tracks. Attacking you directly wouldn't win her any points with Danielle."

"And it was Hailey who had the case with the virus," Gunner reminded him. "I honestly thought it might be her, given her past connections with the anti-government guy."

"Claire even asked me how I wasn't sick when I brought Hailey in. How did I miss that?" Damon was grim as he turned away from his friend and the truth of Martin's statement. Honestly, he hadn't given Hailey another thought, even with the case. She was just young and in love with Travis, that was obvious. He'd never given either woman much thought as an enemy and realized his error. His mama would slap him from the grave if she could for slipping up and believing all the macho nonsense about women being the softer sex. He was a fucking idiot, and it might cost him the woman he loved. Had loved from the moment he'd seen her. It *was* a twin thing.

"She'd better not hurt Dani because, woman or not, I will kill her."

"The CO has been informed, but has his hands full with the rebels. He isn't taking Claire as a threat very seriously," Gunner said.

Damon was scared. They'd all made the same mistake. For the first time in a long time, he was terrified. Because not only was Claire an obsessed psychopath, she was sick. She'd been shaking and sweating when he last saw her. He'd thought at the time it was worry for a friend. But her eyes had also been bloodshot, and not from crying. Thinking back, he knew the answer. Claire was infected.

And she had Dani.

CHAPTER 15

*D*ani followed Claire toward the quarantined tent where she said Hailey was awake and calling for her. She'd been hesitant to leave, but knew Damon could take care of himself, and everyone else if he needed to. Hailey was dying and Dani wanted to be there for her, especially if she was calling out for her.

"Where're you going, Claire? The tent is that way," she said, pointing toward the path that would take them directly there.

She was tired and bruised and knew she'd be needed for all the injured that would be coming in. Dr. Nelson would have his hands full and he'd be splitting his own staff up to deal with the Ebola patients and soldiers coming in with shrapnel, gunshot wounds, and a myriad of other injuries sustained from the explosions that shook the camp.

"I need you to come with me, Dani. Away from everyone else."

"But, why? We don't have time for this," Dani said, her voice sharp with impatience. "Another area needs to be set up for the injured, and we have to begin salvaging supplies from the infirmary. Whatever issue you have can wait, okay?"

Dani turned to head back toward where she'd last seen Damon. More than anything, she needed to see him and make sure he'd been able to get Martin and Anuma out of the shambles they'd been trapped inside.

"Dani," Claire called. "You really should listen to me."

Something in Claire's voice stopped Dani. Goose bumps broke out all over her body, and the hair on the back of her neck stood up. Her internal warning system was going haywire as she slowly turned around. That had never happened with Claire before, but she felt the difference.

"I need to tell you something important," Claire said.

Her voice was devoid of emotion, but it was the gun in her hand that had Dani's attention. The gun that was unsteady but pointed directly at her abdomen. "You have my attention. Why do you have a gun?"

"I knew you wouldn't listen to me otherwise."

"You've always been my friend, Claire. Why wouldn't I listen to you?"

"Because of him, of course. You want to go running back to him." The disgust and hate in her voice was something that chilled Dani and scared her more than the weapon in her hand.

Dani hadn't moved since she'd seen the gun, but Claire motioned her toward the path leading away from the quarantined tent. It was dark where they were. The attack had knocked out some of the power, but Dani was able to distinguish the dirt path that led to the helipad. Why would she want to go there?

But she was willing to cooperate, because even in the dimness of the lights in the distance, Dani could see something was seriously wrong with her friend. "What's wrong, Claire?"

"Walk," she ordered.

Dani turned back around and walked in the direction she was ordered. The brush and jungle growth had been cleared away so her feet didn't snag and trip. She racked her brain to come up with a reason that her best friend was holding a gun to her back and forcing her away from the safety of the camp.

She was also starting to understand what might be wrong with Claire.

When Damon's helicopter came into view, Dani focused on the script scrawled on the nose. *Archangel.* There were lights surrounding the landing zone and it illuminated the area in about a hundred foot radius. For the first time, she saw his nickname and didn't feel the guilt that normally weighed her down. Because Damon had been right, she'd carried around the weight of a failure that wasn't hers to carry. Gabriel had died because he couldn't stay away from helping others, even during a Hemorrhagic Fever epidemic.

Dani walked all the way up and touched his name, and it gave her strength. Claire was infected; it was the only thing that made sense, and it explained the crazed look in her eyes. Whatever she had to say could be blamed on the fever she was likely running.

Turning to face her friend, Dani asked, "What do you want to talk about, my friend?" She kept her voice soft and neutral. And it was an effort because a thin line of blood was running from Claire's left eye down her cheek.

"What if I told you that I did something terrible, but for a noble reason?"

"I would say that I'd like to know what you did and what the reason was."

Claire wiped at the blood, not noticing that it continued to leak out and stain the back of her hand. She'd lowered the gun slightly, but her right hand was shaking badly. "I'm not an evil person," she whispered.

"You've been the one mutating the virus, haven't you?" It was a guess, but the way Claire's eyes widened convinced Dani that she was right. "But why? Make me understand how you could do that? Was it for money? Is someone paying you to weaponize Ebola?"

Claire shook her head, the gun finally dropping to her side. "No. I would never do something like that," she said. Her tone was reasonable, as if the thought of selling the virus for profit was more abhorrent than mutating it in the first place.

"Then, why? Why did that village have to die?"

"Because of you," she suddenly yelled. Her free hand went up to tangle in her hair, pushing the thick mass off her forehead and smearing blood everywhere. "You were going to break up the team, and I wouldn't get to see you again, not the way we get to see each other on deployment."

"But we both live in Atlanta. We wouldn't have stopped being friends just because I wasn't going into the field anymore. We see each other all the time when we aren't on a deployment. And it was just time to step down and let Martin take a turn."

"It wouldn't have been the same."

Dani leaned all the way back against Damon's helicopter. She knew it was only a matter of time before he found her. That's what he was good at, and he'd notice she was missing as soon as he got out of that wreck of a tent. All she had to do was keep Claire talking.

"I think you might be sick, Claire. Your nose is bleeding."

"I'll be fine," she said, and wiped the blood away with the

back of her hand again. "We just have to wait until your fuck buddy gets here."

"Are you talking about Damon? How do you know about us?"

She smirked, but with the drying, darkening blood on her face, it made her look like some kind of macabre clown. "I watched the way you looked at each other and then I saw him go into your tent and send the soldier away to stand watch. I knew what you were doing with him."

"Why does that matter, Claire? I don't understand what's going on," Dani said. She knew she sounded exasperated, but she didn't recognize her friend. She was confessing to something awful just to keep Dani doing fieldwork. But she was clearly sick, so maybe it all made some kind of weird sense to Claire that it didn't for anyone else.

"She's in love with you, Dani. That's what this is about," Damon said, walking forward from the shadows.

Dani looked him over, seeing no signs that he'd been hurt in his rescue efforts. Her shoulders relaxed because he was here, and he would make everything okay. He already had in so many ways. And then his words penetrated. Claire —loved—her?

"So, you finally came," Claire said, as she casually raised the gun and pointed it at him.

"I think you knew I would," he said calmly.

"We both love her, don't we?"

Damon nodded. "Yes, we do. And only one of us gets to have her."

"Claire?" Dani whispered. "Claire." She said it louder to get her friend's attention. "You love me?"

Claire finally stopped glaring at Damon long enough to swing her gaze to Dani's. "I've been in love with you since our first deployment together. Remember? We got drunk on smuggled whiskey and you told me that you were through with men forever. I thought I might have a chance…"

She trailed off and looked back at Damon. "But I didn't, did I? Because out in the world there was always someone who looked like your saint of a husband. I couldn't compete with that, and I knew it. Even then."

"I never knew. I'm sorry, Claire."

Damon hadn't moved, and Dani wasn't happy with how steady Claire suddenly was with the gun in her hand. "Why did you infect the soldiers?"

"To kill me," Damon answered. "Isn't that right? If I was out of the picture, then Dani might reconsider the desk job and continue on the way it always was."

"That's right, lover boy." Her words slurred, but at least the bleeding had stopped for the moment. "I'm surprised you don't have that handy rifle with you. Don't you snipers get off on killing people using a scope and distance? Never being up close and personal unless you're fucking someone."

"Don't worry, Claire. I'll be real close when I kill you."

Dani had never heard Claire speak in such a way. Her words were as crude as the look on her face. She was devolving quickly as the fever spiked and the virus spread to her brain. She'd seen it before in patients with the disease, usually the last stages. They cussed, screamed, or just rambled nonsense as their bodies shut down.

Anger and adrenaline must have been what were keeping Claire on her feet.

And Damon wasn't helping. Claire pulled a syringe from her back pocket. It was loaded with a clear fluid. It was the one missing from the gold case. "How did Hailey get the case?"

"I'd hidden it with her stuff. You know she never checks her things once she's settled in." Claire shrugged. "The little twit found it ahead of schedule. I was supposed to have the staff sergeant with me when I conveniently found it and blamed the whole thing on her."

"I feel like I don't even know you," Dani said.

"But I know you. Everything about you."

Damon finally looked at Dani. He had his stone face on, the one that didn't give away whatever he was planning. But he said, "She's got a little house with a shrine built to you, sugar. Pictures of you sleeping, pictures of you together in different countries, and pictures of you with other people. Claire's been stalking you when she's not with you."

"Stop it," Claire yelled and threw the syringe at him.

Dani watched has he caught it, by reflex. And then she saw Claire swing the gun toward her again. The smile on her face was cruel as she watched them both.

"You have a choice," she said to Damon. "You inject yourself with that syringe, or I shoot the woman we both love. Then, you can kill me. But you won't have her and I will."

"You're sick, Claire. Let me help you," Dani pleaded. "Please, don't do this."

"He's not good enough for you," she said. Her voice was back to that dead tone that signaled she was ready to take action. And then she fired at Dani. The bullet hit the nose of the helicopter next to her. Two inches to the right and that bullet would have been in Dani's stomach.

"Do it now," she demanded.

"Please don't, Damon. Don't do this," Dani said. She was too scared and bewildered to cry. Either way, Claire was going to kill him. Whether it was with a bullet or the virus, Damon was a dead man. And there was nothing she could do to stop it. She was going to lose the man she loved. Again.

Damon smiled and uncapped the needle. "I trust Gunner," he said, right before plunging the needle into his thigh.

"No," Dani screamed and lunged forward toward him.

But he was already moving. Claire's arm had dropped and

started to swing toward him when he pulled the needle out and threw it hard at her face. The instinct to duck was too strong and she did, recovering too late. Damon was on her, twisting her hand into an unnatural position and taking the gun away from her. She sank to her knees, screaming in pain, and then she keeled over and vomited everywhere.

"She's infected," Damon said.

Dani was next to him in an instant. "I know." And it broke her heart. The whole damn thing did. Claire was sobbing, holding her stomach and moaning. Blood was beginning to trickle out of her ears at an alarming rate.

"We need to get her to the quarantine zone."

But Damon shook his head. "She's not going to make it, sugar. Look at all the blood." He pulled Dani close and hugged her tight. "Tell her you love her," he whispered into her hair.

Dani looked up at him in disbelief. "She just tried to kill you." It was something she would have expected from his brother, that overwhelming compassion in the face of what some would call evil. And it was like Gabriel was with them, watching over them both.

Guiding them.

She went down to her knees and pulled Claire into her arms and away from the mess she'd made on the ground. If Damon trusted Gunner enough to inject himself with a full dose of the virus, then she'd trust his serum as well and give Claire what she needed. She couldn't stop herself. And she couldn't process everything that the woman in her arms had done. To Dani, she was still just her best friend. She'd mourn that later and let the anger come then.

"I love you too, Claire. You've been the best thing that's happened in my sad life. You always made me smile, even when I didn't want to." She hugged the crying woman closer. "Thank you for loving me."

"I'm sorry, Dani. So sorry for what I've done."

"Don't worry about that now. We have to get you well, so you can fix it, okay?"

Claire nodded and then relaxed into Dani's arms. Her crying had stopped and she was burning up. She was hotter than a human body should ever be, and when she slumped over, Dani knew it was over.

She looked up at Damon with tears streaking down her face. "Tell me this isn't my fault."

He pulled Claire out of her arms and laid her on the ground, checking for a pulse. He pulled back and shook his head, finding none. "What she did wasn't your fault. She never stopped to think about what her actions would do, beyond keeping you with her."

He pulled her up into his arms and away from the body. Dani shuddered and forced the sob back down, stinging her throat in the process. The hot tears she couldn't stop. For the lost lives of innocent villagers, to the soldiers that were infected at the camp, to the woman who'd loved her and had gone mad because of it.

"I think she used the first syringe on that coma patient and then used the second on herself," he said. "I think the guilt of what she'd done finally caught up with her."

"It doesn't excuse her," Dani sniffed.

"Well, I, for one, am glad the bitch is dead," Gunner snarled, coming into view. He was holding his case, and when he reached them, he grabbed them both and pulled them into a hug. "She almost shot both of you."

"Calm down, man. I had it handled," Damon said.

"You gave yourself a full dose of the virus, dumbass. How am I supposed to react to that?"

"You heard it all?" Dani asked.

"Every little bit. And we got it recorded as a confession of sorts. But since justice has already been served, I guess it doesn't really matter now. But I'm still pissed off."

Gunner was down on one knee, jerking open his case and coming out with another needle. "Since you were so goddamn cavalier about sticking yourself, you won't mind this." And he came up and stabbed Damon in the same thigh that he'd given himself the shot in.

"Ow, you bastard. I didn't actually give myself the shot, just got the needle in as a distraction before pulling it out and throwing it at her. She'd taken a shot at Dani, damn it."

"I don't care, this is another precaution." And then he came up with another syringe. "And one for you, my dear, since you decided to pardon the psychopath with close physical contact."

Dani didn't argue, just presented her arm for the shot. He was a lot gentler with her, even though she could tell he was still pissed. She grabbed his arm and pulled him into a hug. "Thank you, Gunner."

"Thank me by naming your first kid after me, even if it's a girl," he muttered, before he stalked off and into the shadows again with his briefcase.

Dani looked up and Damon and slid her arms around his waist. "I knew you'd find me."

"Gabriel told me where you were."

She pulled back and stared up at him confused. He pointed toward the cockpit. There was a soft blue glow that she hadn't noticed before. "What is that?"

"Motion activated. I sleep in my chopper a lot when I'm on a mission. That glow has saved my ass on several occasions. It's set to go off when anyone gets within a hundred yards of my bird."

"He really is with us, isn't he?"

Damon nodded and kissed her. "He always will be. He

loved you until the day he died, and I will love you until there's not a single breath left in my body."

"I love you, Damon."

"Damn straight, you do. Now, let's get out of here and see if Gunner has singlehandedly saved the camp yet."

"What did he inject us with this time?"

Damon smiled. "The cure."

"That's hard to believe, but it would be a miracle."

"I'd only ever bet against Gunner in poker."

CHAPTER 16

"I quit," Mike Hansen said. "You guys are driving me to drink."

It had been three months since Liberia and all the death that had taken place there and Damon Dupree had never been happier. He was getting married today to the most beautiful woman in the world, and he had his friends by his side. Even the grumpy one.

"You can't quit, Uncle Mike. Daddy says it makes you a sore loser if you quit 'cause you're losing."

"How did you get so good at poker?" Mike grumbled and tossed his cards down.

Xavier Steele pointed his little finger right at Damon, and he couldn't help but grin at the disgruntled look on Mike's face. The kid was fleecing the big man of all his money. Damon couldn't have been prouder of him if he'd been his own son.

Zach was grinning, but not really paying attention because his wife, Elizabeth, had just bent over to adjust the flowers on Jesse's twin girls. Damon rolled his eyes, but

146

understood completely. He didn't think he was that bad, however.

"You are, you know," Jesse said, grinning at him. He nodded toward their friend, still ogling his wife. "When Dani walks by, you can't even string together two words."

"I don't believe you," Damon mumbled and looked back at his hand. He didn't need to, he was sitting on a full house, Aces over Eights. The dead man's hand, but he was alive and well, thanks to Gunner.

"Has anyone heard from Gunner today? Did he make his flight?"

"He'll be here," Zach said. "He's tied up in some debrief that's still going on over his Ebola serum. That whole thing in Liberia has blown up in everyone's faces, especially once that Dr. Graham went on *Larry King Live* about his damn book."

Jesse took the cards out of Xavier's hands and pointed toward Elizabeth. "Your mother wants you." The boy hopped down from his chair, racing off toward his mom. He turned back toward Damon. "How is Hailey doing?"

They all knew the story, and Dani was keeping tabs on her friend. "She's got some organ damage that is going to be slow healing, but she's alive and thankful."

And, even though Dani refused to speak to Travis, and he *had* been fired from his position at the CDC, Dani had quietly helped him get his son into this country and away from his grandfather.

"Gunner took it pretty hard over losing some of those soldiers," Damon said. "He went into his lab and didn't come out until he had a workable serum to inoculate everyone that had been exposed."

Zach shook his head. "He needs a caretaker. Otherwise, that old butler of his is going to find his rotting corpse in that basement of his."

Damon grinned. "He does tend to forget to eat when he's on a project." His cell phone made a chirpy noise and he looked down. He read the text message. "Speak of the devil. He said not to hold the wedding for him, but he'd be at the reception if he had to fly himself. He's ramming his serum down the throats of anyone that will listen to him."

"Good for him," Jesse said.

"No way is the FDA going to approve it until they get their grimy hands on it and decide how to make money on it," Mike added. He was looking at his single dollar left in front of him. "Your son," he said to Zach, "is a poker shark."

"He makes me proud," Zach laughed.

"Well, I'd better go tell Red that we can finally get this done."

Jesse was the one rolling his eyes this time. "For the love of God, Damon, don't phrase it like that or she'll never marry you."

"She's crazy about me. And my daddy has a shotgun and a pet alligator; both will be used to get her back into the family if needed."

Then he left his friends to find his soon-to-be bride. He took the stairs two at a time and went into their room without knocking. And what he saw took his breath away. She was in nothing but a tiny lacy something that didn't hide anything from his hungry gaze, white stockings with garters, and white heels.

"You are not supposed to see the bride before the wedding," she scolded playfully. "It's bad luck."

"I make my own luck, and I think I'm damned lucky to catch you in that little number." He slammed the door and locked it before stalking over to his redheaded beauty. She had her hands on her hips and a sassy look on her face.

She held a hand up and pressed it against his chest. "You are going to ruin my make-up."

He leaned in; just close enough to kiss, but not. "You can fix it again."

"My daddy and yours are downstairs right now," she squeaked, dodging his kiss.

"Then it can be a shotgun wedding if they find out."

The love of his life pressed her delectable body against his and wound her hands around his neck. "Maybe if we're real quiet," she said suggestively.

She was wearing some kind of sultry perfume that had him putting his nose into the crook of her neck to inhale her. Dani smelled like sunshine and sex, and it was making his pants tight and uncomfortable. He nibbled and she sighed, sliding her nails against his scalp to urge him on.

And then the door opened. Lily Calhoun and Elizabeth Steele stood there with their arms crossed over their chests, both trying, and failing, to look disapproving. The big grins were a giveaway.

"Out," Lily said, glaring at Damon. "You are needed downstairs by the fathers, who saw you sneaking up here, by the way." She held up the spare key. "Daddy Dupree gave me this and said to give you some hell."

"And we need to help Dani get dressed," Elizabeth said with a grin. "You can help her undress later; I promise."

"Okay, okay," he said, hands raised and backing out. As much as he would've enjoyed a quickie before the actual nuptials, he wanted her to be his wife before he made love to her again. "I love you, Red. See you downstairs in thirty minutes. I'll be the one in front waiting anxiously."

He watched the love shine out of her eyes as she smiled at him. "I'll be there."

And he went out and closed the door behind him. Then he went into his brother's room and sat down on the bed. Even after all these years, the room still smelled like his brother. Nothing had been moved or changed either. It wasn't a shrine, but it didn't feel empty and cold either. Damon wanted some time alone with his twin. He was quiet for a long time, collecting his thoughts and letting his brother's presence infuse his soul. Damn, he missed him. His other half.

"Thank you, Gabe. For bringing her into our lives," he said. He had a photo in his hands. The one of himself and Gabriel, with Dani in the middle smiling into the camera. The way it was, and the way it always would be. The three of them together. Only Gabriel was watching over them and Damon felt that he would be happy for them both.

"I'll take care of her, I promise."

With his head bowed, he heard her, but didn't see her. He must have lost track of time because when he looked up and saw Dani in her wedding gown, she stole his breath. She touched his cheek and rubbed her thumb softly over his lips. There were no tears on her face, only love and understanding.

"We'll take care of each other."

"Forever," he whispered. It was a vow that he'd keep for the rest of their lives.

ALSO BY KORI DAVID

In Zach's Arms (Once a Marine, Always a Marine - Book 1)

Lily's Outlaw (Once a Marine, Always a Marine - Book 2)

Shelby's Secret (Once a Marine, Always a Marine - Book 4)